# CONTENTS

# THE ELEVATOR WASN'T MOVING
## FAST ENOUGH

The elevator wasn't moving fast enough. I watched the dull red numbers change from floor to floor, seven, eight... They seemed to be moving slower, almost like the building was getting tired. A four letter word caught in my throat. I would have let it loose if I were alone. There were two others on the slow ride, a rich gray suit and a bicycle courier. I swallowed the word and began tapping my foot, thinking the elevator may get annoyed and move faster.

The suit got off on nine, slowing me down even more. I moved over to the panel and smacked the close door button a couple of times which seemed to amuse the courier. The button was useless. The elevator doors closed in their own sweet time. After an interminable wait, it began to rise again.

"Running late?" The courier asked. I turned, about to snap at him. He was young, probably couldn't drink legally. He was fairly trim but rather sloppy in the hygiene department. It looked he lost his razor a few days ago.

"Yes," I replied, turning back to the console to watch the numbers slowly change. There was no need to bite his head off.

"Can you push twelve, please?" The courier asked.

"We just past it," I said and pushed the button.

"I'm not late," The courier said smiling. I turned back quickly to the young man. Young was relative since I just had my twenty-fifth birthday. He stood confidently in his black knee length bike shorts, his windbreaker unzipped open to his stomach, revealing a taut blue t-shirt. It was the nicest thing anyone had done for me in a long time. He was not as shabby as I first thought.

"Thank you," I said as pleasant as I could. It was hard, as late as I was, to muster a smile, but I did. A lot of stress faded away at that moment. Here was a little piece of the world that wasn't out to get me. It would be nice if he was a few years older with a better job. Not that my job was anything to be proud about. My father's death had wounded me in heart and future. It created a legal mountain whose peak wouldn't be reached until my thirty-second birthday. I was rich, I just couldn't touch any of it.

"No problem," The courier replied, then he leaned against the far wall and looked away, seemingly uninterested in more conversation. For a moment, I thought I would have to fend off an advance. I looked down at my blouse and skirt to see if there was a stain. Nothing. Just me. A strange disappointment clouded my mind. I would have preferred a small flirtation.

The elevator doors opened on fifteen. I sighed and exited, the courier seemingly oblivious to my leaving. "Good luck," the courier said when my back was turned. I turned as the elevator doors closed. He smiled at me in a soft dreamy way. Unthinkingly, I smiled back, the doors acting as a comfortable shield for the brief flirtation. Life was good again.

"Ella, you're late again," Agnus Tremaine spat with hands on her wide hips. Her graying hair, glued in curled clumps atop her head, bounced to emphasize every word. I sighed. I had hoped to escape my step mother's notice. Life was bad again.

"Accident on sixth street," I stated as I moved toward the utility room. My utility room, held in trust.

2

"My daughters don't seem to have a problem arriving on time," Agnus continued with a grating tone. I hated these times. Seven more years of being under this woman's claws.

"They seem to be on vacation more than not," I returned with my own venom. Agnus had fooled my father into tieing up his assets until I was older. She, of course, became executor and, in turn, my jailer. I suspected she was a slut in bed. I could think of no other reason my father would screw me like he had. I loved him more than anyone, but he was a man and I knew he wrote that will with his dick.

"Business trips are not vacations," Angus defended Drizella and Anastasia. I was sure they got little done in Tahiti with my money. "I only wish you had their work ethic," she continued as if I didn't know the truth.

I ignored her continuing rants and pulled out the bucket and mop. My bucket and my mop. I was required to stay with Tremaine Marketing, Inc until I came into my inheritance. He just failed to say in what capacity. Agnus thought it best I was the night janitor. Seven more years and I can fire her. I began to fill the bucket with hot water. At least Agnus would go home soon. My home.

"The floors were done poorly last night," Agnus continued while pointing out some corners that held dust. There was a rider in the will that stated if I failed to stay with the firm, I would lose it to the next in line. Agnus was next in line. My only saving grace was that she had to answer to a board and the court. My life was miserable, but I still had hope.

I added a potent lemon-scented cleaning fluid to the bucket. At least it overwhelmed the perfume that Agnus liked to swim in. I ignored her other admonishments, knowing they were designed to get me to lose it and quit. That wasn't going to happen. I just had to stay out of trouble and in seven years, I get to fire the bitch.

I turned with my prepared bucket and smiled at Agnus. It was my you'll-get-yours smile. She never understood that smile. I think she thought I had a few screws loose. It always made her back away and lose her train of thought. The only attack I was allowed. I certainly couldn't yell at the CEO. That might be grounds for termination. It was a war and I had to let her win all the early battles.

"Good evening Mrs. Tremaine, Ella," Raj said, his olive-skinned smile leading the way out of the elevator. I smiled back, which irritated Agnus more. She had hired Raj as the night tech thinking I wouldn't be comfortable with an immigrant from India. The opposite occurred. He had become a dear friend and I adopted myself into his family. His wife Kiran and their daughter Aanya were such a lovely family.

"Mr. Vijaya, do think it is wise spending your time with pleasantries when there is work to be done?" Agnus asked. Raj lost his smile. His green card held him to his job as surely as the will held me.

"No, Mrs. Tremaine," Raj answered and moved quickly to the control room. I wanted so much to shove the end of my mop into Agnus's mouth to shut her up. I closed my eyes and let the image float away. Seven more years. Raj could stay. Agnus was out.

Agnus followed Raj into the control room. I was sure it was to give him an impossible list of tasks and remind him not to fraternize with the janitorial staff. The hallway seemed to brighten when she left. A devious thought entered my mind and I laughed to myself. The first sign of insanity, but it felt good. I began mopping. Mopping exactly where Agnus would have to walk in order to leave. Images of her falling on her ass were pleasant. I started humming Dancing Queen and used the mop as my partner. My thoughts were very pleasant.

Agnus didn't fall. I apologized for not thinking and starting at that end of the hall. It was humorous watching her walk in her high heels while holding herself along the wall. It was hard to hold my smile in, but I had a lot of practice at it. The corners of my mouth stayed low while my insides jumped with glee.

"Good night, Agnus," I called as she pushed the elevator button. She hated when I called her by her first name at work. I saw the anger in her eyes when she turned. I knew she wasn't going to walk back across the newly mopped floor again. Chalk up another one for Ella. Agnus just grimaced and stepped into the elevator. My body relaxed when the doors closed. The bitch was gone.

I pushed the bucket and mop into the corner. It was usually the last thing I did. I had a system. A series of steps that optimized the time it would take to clean the offices. Mopping first would just slow me up. Optimized work time allowed for optimized free time. I grabbed the large wheeled garbage can, vacuum cleaner and dust rag. Office to office, I quickly dusted, emptied trash, and vacuumed then closed the door.

I had told Agnus it took thirty minutes to clean an office. She said I should be able to do it in twenty. It actually took less than five when I put my mind to it. Chalk up another one for Ella. I was done in under three hours, floors mopped and all the glass cleaned. They were my offices, so it wasn't as hard to do as Agnus thought. She was conniving, but a little on the dumb side. If she really wanted to get on my nerves, she should have me working during the day, with her.

I restored all my supplies and cleaned myself up a bit. I tossed a few dollars at the vending machines for a coke and chips. I went to the control room to see Raj. It was our nightly ritual. Raj worked and I kept him company. It was a somewhat boring existence, yet when shared, it lost its 'boring' status and become tolerable.

"Almost a record, Ella," Raj said, pointing at the clock.

"If she wouldn't have hung around, I would have broken it," I said. I raced myself every night. The quicker I got done, the sooner I could chat with Raj. I watched as he executed another batch process. The screen said he was updating the report server. A restructured database that allowed quick access for decision-makers. The two years I have sat with Raj had schooled me well on the inner workings of my company. I don't think Agnus thought I knew thing one about the goings one. Chalk up another one.

"Kiran wants you to come over Saturday afternoon," Raj said when he was sure the batch was executing. He spun in his chair to look at me. They were using me to try and become more American. I loved them, so I always agreed.

"I would love too," I agreed, "is Kiran making those potato things again?" They were to die for.

"Aloo kikki," Raj reminded me. I will never remember the name, "of course she will." Saturday seemed to far off. My social life was shit when I wasn't with the Vijayas. Working nights puts a huge cramp in one's mojo. I sleep when most people were awake and was heading off to work when they are getting frisky. I was sure that was part of Agnus's plan.

"I have to warn you," Raj continued, "Aanya has a new board game she wishes to play." I laughed. Aanya thought of me as a big sister. In truth, I thought of her as my little sister. She was more attuned to American styles than I and schooled me often. I helped her with the things a young girl couldn't talk to her parents about. Usually, boy things. Aanya was in the eighth grade and the drama had begun. The boys were just beginning to think girls weren't as useless as they thought. Girls, on the other hand, were separating the studs from the duds.

"Sounds like fun," I said. I had no plans that even sounded close to a good board game. Raj looked at me funny. I could tell he was think-ing. His eyes always became still when his brain was working.

"I love that you come," Raj said, "it makes Kiran and Aanya very happy, but I worry we are stopping you from things." I smiled and decided to torture him.

"What kind of things?" I asked.

"You know...things," Raj said, using his hands to emphasize things.

"You mean like snorkeling?" I asked with humor.

"You know what I mean," Raj replied, trying to hide his blush.

"Ahh, you mean wild sex," I said, my eyes wide waiting to see if I could deepen the red in his cheeks.

"Well..." Raj stuttered, "I mean you're a pretty girl. You should be out on dates." Raj tried hard to clean up my words. I smiled at him.

"Agnus makes that difficult," I said, "my time is coming." Seven more years. Raj turned back to his terminal and began typing again.

"Kiran worries about you," Raj said quietly. I felt my heart throb. Raj was worried about me. I loved him for it. I was in a hole right now and in seven years, I would climb out.

"You tell Kiran that all I need is aloo kikki," I said with a little laughter. That got me a chuckle. I certainly didn't want Raj sad on my account. I thought back to my last boyfriend. It had been before my father had past away. I would be lying to myself if I didn't admit that I missed the intimacy. Sex had its medicinal properties and was a ton of fun as well. Fried potatoes and board games were a poor substitute.

I changed the subject and asked Raj what he was doing. This is how I learned about my company. Raj, who had access to all the information, would instruct me in his tasks and I, in turn, would learn. I knew an awful lot about how the money moved, who moved it and why. I knew each employee, who were the slackers and who drove the business. In seven years, the board wouldn't find a naive girl, they would see a knowledgeable woman owner who knew how things worked. Agnus was digging her own grave. That was my solace.

I stepped into the bathroom before the end of my shift. I looked into the mirror and began to dishevel myself. I pulled a few strands of hair from my ponytail and let them float in a wispy mess. I smudged my glasses with fingerprints and pulled my shirt so it hung poorly, half out of my skirt. I had to look harried before Agnus arrived. There was rarely a need for her to be at work early. Her sole goal was to ascertain my level of misery. I gave her the answer she wanted to see. I girl on her last leg, about to throw away her inheritance. My secret defiance was my shield. Only seven years to go.

~

The drive home was miserable. Bands of rain ran across the windshield with a ferocity that made that wipers moot. I decide to pull over and let it pass. My first mistake. I ran over something that must have been placed there just for me. The telltale flapping and the steering pulling to the right let me know I had a flat. I went through my entire vocabulary of foul words. Then, I went through the litany again. The rain picked up. I made up some new words.

I waited for the rain to stop. I used the time wisely and pulled the owner's manual from the glove compartment. I had never replaced a tire on this car. I cringed when I saw the instructions. There was a bolt in the trunk, when turned, lowered a temporary tire. It was raining and I would have to retrieve it from under the car. The rain never stopped, but did change to something less than a deluge. I sighed and stepped out into the rain.

There were a lot of places I could have picked to pull over. I had to pick a spot where recent construction had left mud where rock should have been. The state had decided it would be good week to dig up the culverts along the side of the road and had deposited most of it on the shoulders. My white tennies sunk on contact. I slammed the door with anger as my only umbrella, I squished my way to the trunk.

I promptly squished my way back when I realized I had not undone the trunk hatch. The world was attacking and my mind was becoming traitorous. I gave up trying to walk carefully when I felt the mud ooze into my socks. Shoes ruined. Chalk one up for mother nature.

The bolt was stubborn. I had no idea which way to turn it as rain pelted my back. Finally, when I felt cold wetness find more private areas, I figured out it was clockwise. I gave up trying to do it quickly. I was soaked. It didn't matter how long it took anymore. I squatted down, my wet skirt fighting the movement, and saw the tire lying in the mud, almost two feet under the car. I tried to reach it, flailing at the edges. I sighed and dropped my knee into the mud. It found the rocks under the mud causing more wonderful words to escape my throat. I cringed as I shifted my knee and created a semi-unpainful spot to anchor it.

One hand on the trunk, I lowered myself, reached under the car and dragged the now muddy tire toward the back. My blouse was ruined by the time I figured out how to detach the tire from the cable that had held it under the car. I carefully lifted, trying to hold it away from my skirt. I turned and a wave of water, mud and whatever else was on the road covered me as a semi passed. I looked down at my clothes and lost it. I was tired, wet and now covered in mud. Swear words were no longer enough. Tears mixed with rain as I slipped and slid my way to the flat front tire. My throat was spasming as I went back for the jack and tire wrench.

Another bout of hard rain whipped through and my left foot slipped into the culvert. It came back missing its shoe. I leaned against the car, clutching the tools, trying to stop the horrid feelings coursing through me. I had no more anger to rely on, only hopelessness.

"You look like you could use some help," a male voice called. I looked up, my glasses blinded by rain. I didn't know who it was. I could only sob, covered in mud and show my tools. I didn't want to be helpless, but my mind was surrendering to it all. You can't fight the world.

"We'll start with the jack," the man said, and took it from my hands. He was taller than me, that much I could tell. He moved confidently to the front as another dousing came from the clouds. I followed him, my sock trying to leave itself in the mud. "Stand away from the side in case it slips," he said as he kneeled into the mud trying to find a secure place for the jack.

"Thank you," I said, remembering my manners. "Thank you," I said louder, certain that my first attempt was lost in the rain. He looked back at me and I saw a smile between the droplets running down my lenses.

"Wrench," he said, holding out his hand. I put the wrench in it and he affixed it to the jack. He began raising the car. "Crappy day for a flat tire," he observed. I nodded though he wasn't looking at me as he concentrated on the jack. I wiped my glasses with my wet finger. He had dark hair, soaked through. His shirt and pants were a mess now but looked expensive. The one shoe I could see was brown leather and not something found at Walmart. My savior was some kind of executive, probably on his way to work. I sucked in a breath and forced my helplessness away.

"That should do it," he said rising with the wrench. I took it from his hands, trading it for a smile.

"Thank you," I said again. I couldn't believe I had lost it. An executive doesn't collapse at the first sign of trouble. In seven years, I needed to be a rock of confidence. He smiled back, the rain running off his nose and past his strong chin.

"You lost your shoe," he said, pointing at my sock.

"It's been one of those days," I said, trying to ignore the loss. I moved to the tire and inserted the blade end of the wrench into the slot of the hubcap as the manual had said. It popped off and I pretended it didn't surprise me. He was there to catch it before slid into the culvert. He watched as I went at the first lug nut. I pushed down on the wrench and it didn't want to move. Hesitantly, his hand moved next to mine and we pushed together. The nut relented. He removed his hand and let me finish.

He stood there in the rain, holding the hubcap and collected lug nuts one at a time. To be honest, his presence gave me strength. His desire not to push the poor woman out of the way and do it himself was nice. He moved from savior to helper without a thought. I was smiling when I finished the last lug nut.

"I'm Ella," I said as I handed him the last nut. The rain was beginning to let up again.

"Peter," he responded.

"Thank you for stopping," I repeated again. I lifted the tire off the car and it bounced in the mud. I longer cared about the mud that splattered on my ankles.

"You said that already," Peter said. I looked up at him. He was smiling at me, almost laughing as I struggled to wheel the flat tire off to the side. He made no move to help, which was strangely helpful. I lifted the dinky donut tire and struggled it onto the bolts. He moved behind me. I suspected he meant to catch me if I started to slide into the culvert. Most helpful.

He handed the nuts to me, one at a time, and I screwed them on hand tight. The rain was beginning to cooperate and became more of drizzle. He handed the wrench back to me and I cranked the lug nuts tight. I turned to seem him loading the flat tire in the trunk. No communication, just optimized performance that limited the time we needed to be in the rain. I liked Peter.

I moved to the front of the car, inserted the wrench into the jack and began undoing what Peter had done. He met me there and watched as the car came down. "You handled that well," he said. I could hear the humor in his voice. He was having fun with me. I laughed.

"I am glad you stopped," I admitted as the jack slowly folded back to its rest position, "I was letting it get to me for a moment there." I looked up as I detached the wrench. He held out his hand and I put the wrench in it. I grabbed the jack and we carried them back to the trunk and threw them in. He closed the trunk and turned to me.

"I think you need to rush home, Ella," Peter said, with a sly smile. I wasn't sure what he meant. Was he giving me a command. I don't take well to commands. His smile changed when he saw my confusion. He leaned closer.

"I think you are a bit more beautiful than you intend right now," Peter said, his smile growing again. I stepped back as the realization hit me. I looked down and quickly covered my breasts. The rain had made my blouse and bra see-thru. The cold rain had woken my nipples. Traitors. Peter laughed sweetly as he backed toward his car. "Absolutely beautiful," he repeated as he opened the door car. A sleek black Lexus that he seemed to fit into well. Red-faced, I headed back to my car and put my soaking wet muddy body on my clean seats.

I looked in the rearview mirror and saw him there. Peter was waiting to make sure I got back on the road. I smiled. Beautiful he said. He looked pretty good himself. I smiled to the world and waved to Peter as I got back on the road. Beautiful. I liked my breasts being beautiful. Thank God I didn't know him. I wouldn't have been able to ever face him again. That was, by far, the best worst experience I ever had. That smile of his was so honest. He wasn't just trying to make me feel good. He meant it. My breasts just got promoted to my favorite body part. Sorry calves, you just got demoted.

~

*J* had Kiran nearly in tears she was laughing so hard. My flat tire exploit was funny now that it was history. Lost a skirt, blouse, and one shoe (therefore two) in the incident. It cost me money I could hardly afford to get the tire repaired, not to mention the sleep I lost. At least my breasts were beautiful. That's the part Kiran thought was best. Thankfully, Raj and Aanya were in the other room while I helped Kiran in the kitchen. Raj would be embarrassed for me and not see the compliment I saw. Kiran understood. She had a wonderful sexy side that she usually only let Raj see when the lights were down. She trusted me, so I knew some of her secrets.

"I told you," Kiran said, between gasps, "you have it going on." Another bout of laughter caught her as she imagined me nearly naked on the side of the road.

"It was kind of nice, " I agreed, "embarrassing, but I think he really thought I was hot."

"You need more flat tires," Kiran laughed, "maybe wear a bikini next time." I tried to hold back my smile, but I just couldn't. It felt good to be admired, if only for a few minutes. I wasn't an exhibitionist, that I knew. It was just his smile and his words. "You should have gotten his number," Kiran added.

"No," I said, "I couldn't. I would die of embarrassment if I ever saw him again."

"He said you were beautiful, " Kiran countered, "and you said he wasn't hard on the eyes." I pushed Kiran's shoulder, lovingly.

"He's probably married," I argued, "what are you are trying to do? Turn me into a slut." Kiran gave me a sly smile.

"A man tells you, you are beautiful, you can at least see if he is married," Kiran raised her eyebrows up and down. Raj had his hands full with this one. I chuckled and held back my response. There was no arguing sex with her.

"You need to take some risks," Kiran continued, "I did with Raj and never regretted it. He is a good father and keeps the bed very warm." Her smile told me exactly what she meant.

"I think you took the last good man, Kiran," I said, half meaning it, "the rest are married, gay, or after only one thing." I wouldn't mind that one thing, but a possible future would be a requirement.

"You need to stop spending your Saturdays here," Kiran said, "you need to put yourself out there." She smiled, "maybe enter a few wet t-shirt contests." We laughed together as we began putting the fried potato patties on the serving tray. I had already forgotten the name of the things. My tongue loved them, it was my brain that refused to cooperate.

After a nice dinner, we all sat down for Aanya's board game. It was different from any other game I had ever played. It turned out to be a very enjoyable game. It was called Stone Age and you had to lead your people from a hunter-gather society to an agrarian one. You did this by gathering resources with workers and dice. You then spent the resources to buy huts and special cards. It was easy to learn and engrossing. Raj won the first game and we all agreed to play another. I thought I had the second game in the bag, but Aanya won by two points. She had amassed a good collection of cards. I would have been upset, but the look on her face was wonderful. She was young and needed the victory. It made the game all the better.

Aanya complained when her mother told her it was time for bed. I gave her a hug and promised to play her game again next week. I was actually looking forward to it. I think I had a strategy down that would lead me to victory. She kissed her mother and father goodnight. I watched the affection and was slightly jealous. I wanted what they had. I wanted crazy passion with a man followed by a family filled with love. I didn't think that was too much to ask for.

Raj broke out a bottle of wine. He and I were just entering our normal work cycle so we were wide awake. Kiran struggled to stay with us during the weekends. I always left when her yawns exceeded more than one a minute. We talked about American things. TV, thank the gods for the DVR, movies, books and anything that made them feel more like citizens. As the night wore down, the topic usually returned to work. That is when Kiran would begin to yawn.

"Your mother was especially upset last night," Raj said, remembering Agnus's tirade about the trash cans not being washed out. I just emptied them since they all had liners.

"She is just trying to wear me down," I said, "it will take more than trash cans to get under my skin." I took a sip of my wine. They both knew that the company was mine as long as I could hold out until I was thirty-two. "Why do you stick around Raj," I said and quickly qualified, "I would hate to lose my only friend there, but she treats you like crap." Kiran and Raj exchanged a look I didn't recognize. I was missing something.

"My staying here in America requires I keep this job," Raj said, "I don't have a choice."

"Is India that bad?" I asked. It didn't seem so horrible. I had even considered visiting there when I came into my inheritance. If Raj and Kiran were examples of the people there, I definitely wanted to make the trip. Kiran's face lost its happiness. I had asked something I shouldn't have.

"My family would not cherish my return," Kiran said, "they think I am dirty now." I saw a sadness in her. I didn't like how it looked.

"I am not the same caste as Kiran," Raj said. Kiran scooted over and leaned on Raj. I had asked something very sensitive. "she married below her status and it is just not done in her family." He paused for a moment before he continued. "Her family holds with the old ways. She and Aanya would be at risk if we were to return." I sucked in my breath. I didn't know there were places in the world where things like that still mattered.

"I didn't know," I said in a way of an apology.

"How could you," Kiran said with a forced smile. I had visions of Kiran and Aanya dragged off to some horrible family tribunal.

"To America," I said, raising my glass "and your quick path to citizenship." Raj smiled and Kiran's smile lost its fakeness. We tapped our glasses together and I quickly changed the subject. The rest of the evening went with less drama and returned to our own brand of humor. I needed them for my sanity and they needed me for a friend. It was a good arrangement. I left when Kiran's yawns exceeded the prescribed parameters.

～

$\mathcal{I}$ was early for once. It was nice to avoid Agnus's admonishments. I was surprised to not find her waiting for me with new degrading instructions on her lips. I took it as a gift and moved to my closet and began retrieving my supplies. I didn't see myself cleaning offices for the rest of my life, but it didn't take a lot of thought and allowed my mind to drift. Lately, it drifted to a man named Peter. Every time I saw that smile in my mind it sent champagne bubbles through my blood.

"What will I wear?" I heard it from my stepmother's office. It sounded like Drizella. I quietly moved down the hall. It was rare to find one of my step sisters at the office anywhere near closing time.

"We'll go shopping," Angus announced with an excited voice, "for both of you." I heard a duet of agreements and knew that both of my sisters were there. I walked into the office, my curiosity getting the best of me. Sure enough, what constituted my family was gathered in Agnus's office.

"Shopping?" I said. I knew it didn't mean me. I liked the tinge of guilt I could generate in them. They may be gold diggers, but they were human as well. I watched their expressions of joy dissipate as their eyes found me. Chalk another one up for Ella. It was going to be a good night.

"This doesn't concern you," Agnus threw back. She was using my inheritance so I felt it did.

"Sounds like a party," I said with an excited grin. I looked to my sisters and they lit up, foolishly thinking I was sharing with them.

"Charity cotillion," Anastasia blurted out. It was so easy to stir her red haired covered brains. I looked back at Agnus who was trying to feign disinterest.

"I suppose we are making a donation," I commented. I made sure the word 'we' was emphasized. Agnus looked flustered. I knew instantly that this was more a society play than a business decision. She had a high opinion of herself and her two daughters.

"It is beneficial for us to contribute back to the community," Agnus lied. She was trying to get her daughters married off to wealthy men. Maybe find another one for herself. More of my money down the drain. Anyone willing to marry those two, wouldn't be rich for long.

"Everybody who's anybody will be there," Anastasia added.

"What's the charity?" I asked. I almost threw my dust rag at Agnus when she had to look it up on the invitation. Beneficial for the company my ass.

"Children's hospital," Agnus read. At least my money wasn't being thrown in a ditch. I felt a little better. I decided I would make Agnus uncomfortable anyway.

"Where's my invitation?" I asked. It was fun watching her fumble with her mind. She was spending my money after all. She didn't see it that way, but I did.

"We need executives to represent the company," Agnus smiled when the answer came to her, "janitorial staff would not be how we would want to represent ourselves." I smiled back and watched her lean away. She hated my smile. Seven more years.

I left them, curses dying on my lips, and returned to my cleaning. It infuriated me that they were using my company to further their gold-digging plans. I almost swore at my father for leaving me in such a predicament. I sucked it back. He was only human and had little defense against a demon like Agnus.

Agnus and her daughters left shortly after. They were babbling about tomorrow's shopping. Executives my ass. I was in an especially dark mood when I sat down with Raj later that night. Even my glasses seemed to be steamed up.

"Why don't you go?' Raj asked me after I had explained my mood.

"Psst," I spat, "me at a formal dance. I couldn't afford to look in the front door. Agnus keeps the purse strings tight about my neck." Raj turned back to his terminal and began typing. He turned back around with wide eyes.

"$5,000 a plate," Raj said, "your sisters better have a good time."

"$5,000?" I exclaimed. Raj nodded. "That bitch. I will be lucky if there is anything left when she's done."

"Why don't you go?" Raj repeated.

"Where would I get $5,000?" I asked, waving at the atmosphere, "I could barely afford to get my tire fixed. Agnus certainly won't give it to me." Raj smiled and went back to his terminal. I moved behind him to see why he was so pleased with himself. His fingers were moving quickly as he fired off some program I had never seen.

"How many tickets do you want?" Raj asked. His voice was arrogant and full of pride. I saw a series of text prompts followed by commands I did not understand.

"What are you doing?" I asked.

"I am in the organizers database," Raj said, "I can slip in a ticket for you and no one would be any wiser." He was exceptionally proud of himself.

"You hacked the system?" I asked. The thought scared me. I took a step back as if that would make it less wrong.

"No one will know," Raj said, "I wrote a program that finds its way into networks." I stared at him. I thought I knew him. "I've never used it before, but it's untraceable." He chuckled to himself, "these people are good. Shark firewall, but I chewed through it in under five seconds."

"Raj!" I said, "you could end up in jail." He shook his head.

"They've never seen anything like this," Raj praised himself, "It travels through so many proxies it's untraceable. That's if they figure out I was in at all."

"Why would you write such a thing?" I had a whole new opinion of him. It was scarier.

"I toy with all sorts of code," Raj explained, "once I get my citizenship, I am going to need a resume. This will be the cornerstone. I am a master of network security. This proves it. Shark firewalls are the best in the business. The same ones the military uses."

"You're risking too much, Raj," I said, "you'll never get your citizenship if you get caught."

"I'm careful," Raj said, but I noticed he ended the code's execution.

"Thanks, but I prefer you out of prison, " I said with a smile, happy he turned off his hacking program. Raj smiled back with a bit of hesitancy. I don't think he thought the whole thing through. Writing the code was as far as his mind took him. He had such a brilliant mind. I think Kiran married up, not down.

The rest of the evening went as the hundred before it. I learned a little more about the company while sharing a nice conversation. The cotillion left my thoughts and hopefully Raj's.

$\sim$

*M*y drive home was dry and without a flat tire. I arrived home to find my sister's already awake. It was odd to see them up before seven. I usually made it a point to be in my room when their alarms began to sing at seven thirty.

"Do you think he will be there?" Drizella asked. Anastasia was leaning on the counter in the kitchen sipping on a cup of tea nodding.

"Of course he'll be there," Anastasia replied, "his family runs the thing."

"Good-looking and loaded," Drizella smiled, "we should research him. Find out what he likes. I sure wouldn't mind walking down the aisle with him." My interest was pi*q*ued. I almost wanted to call the poor guy and warn him.

"You'll have to go through me first," Anastasia warned, her red hair waving from side to side as she bobbed her head. "You wouldn't have even known about him if it wasn't for me." Drizella looked like she might fight back, but instead, became thoughtful for a moment.

"We can't go upset with each other," Drizella reasoned, "he'll hate us both. No one wants bickering sisters." Anastasia's face softened. "he has to have rich friends. If we play nice, the winner can set up the other with his friends." A smiled grew on Anastasia's face. It was mirrored on Drizella's. I hated when they laughed together. It sounded like a clutch of chickens with breathing problems. I moved in to save my ears.

"Who are you two after now?" I said as I entered. Anastasia was startled, which pleased me. Drizella just smiled. It looked like her mother's smile. It displeased me.

"You wouldn't know him," Drizella said with a sweetness coating her bitter undertones.

"Try me," I said.

"You know the Charmings?" Anastasia asked, "the one's throwing the charity cotillion?" I nodded though I had no idea who they were. High society was lost on me.

"They have a son," Drizella continued, "he's single, wealthy, and not hard on the eyes." Anastasia chuckled. Another chicken chuckle.

"And you two are going to throw yourselves at him," I observed. Inside I was laughing. He would have to be a complete idiot to connect with either of my step sisters. It would almost be worth the $5,000 just to watch.

"Throw is the wrong word, dear sister," Drizella corrected, "we are not without charm."

"Certainly not," Agnus agreed. She came in behind me and made me jump. I hate when she does that. "and we have to go shopping to make sure he sees those charms."

"I thought this was business related," I said, my tone dropped to my disgusted level.

"Two birds, my dear, two birds," Agnus said. She moved to the coffee pot and poured herself one. "Would you like a cup, Ella?" She always offered me things she knew I would decline. I was on my way to bed and in no need of caffeine. I choose not to respond.

"You can't use company funds to marry off your daughters," I said. I shouldn't have, but she was spending my inheritance in the most irritating way. Agnus just smiled at me and sipped her coffee. She knew she could. "How does hounding the son of the benefactors improve Tremaine Marketing's image?" I was getting angry. I should have just gone to bed.

"It is all a little above your head, dear," Agnus continued. More chicken giggles from her daughters. "It's best to leave the complexity to those who understand it." My face began to heat up. I had to remind myself that she held the purse strings for seven more years.

"You look like you can use some sleep, dear," Agnus continued. She took a sip of her coffee and seemed pleased watching me stew. "Jealousy doesn't become you," Agnus added. It was all I could do to not scream. They were in my house, working at my company, and spending my money. There wasn't a damn thing I could do about it.

"Seven years, Agnus," I said slowly. I was grinding my teeth.

"That's a really long time, sweetie." Agnus's grin was unbearable. I almost let loose of the 'B' word. I knew it would be costly if I did. I took a deep breath and gave her the smile see disliked so much instead. At least it removed hers. I headed off to bed, my mind fuming at my father for leaving me in such a mess.

～

*I* hardly slept at all that day. It is hard enough to keep your eyes closed when the sun is out. Add in a controlling stepmother that boiled my brain and sleep was the last thing my mind wanted to do. Instead of counting sheep, I thought of many wonderful methods of torture for Agnus. When it was time for work again, I was exhausted, angry, and less than friendly.

I stepped off the elevator on time. Agnus was waiting with a list of todos. I think she saw me near the breaking point. I kept to my smile and half listened to her demands. She became flustered halfway through, seeing that I wasn't going to lose it. We exchanged veiled unpleasantries and headed our separate ways. Without my surrender, the war would rage for another seven years.

"Bad day?" Raj asked. I had sat down rather hard and I think I was glowering.

"I am letting her get to me," I sighed, "I have to watch her trash my future and there is nothing I can do about it. Now she wants to trade some of my future so her daughters can fish for husbands." I chuckled when I thought about it. "It's not like they have a chance anyway."

"They do come off a bit needy," Raj agreed.

"A bit greedy," I corrected. Raj laughed then covered his mouth with his hand. He was never one to loudly disparage someone else. Anything above a whisper made him uncomfortable. His stalled laugh did make me feel better. At least someone in the world understood my troubles.

"I still think you should attend the cotillion," Raj said after he brought himself under control, "you need to get out and meet people and rescue your sister's poor targets." This time, I laughed while shaking my head no.

"Even if we could get away with it, I couldn't short the children's hospital $5,000," I responded. The thought of me running around warning men of my sisters approach was amusing. I could see Rag was disappointed in my choice. "You just want to use your new toy," I observed.

"For good. It must never be used by the dark side," Raj joked, "I can think of nothing more honorable than putting you on the dance floor where you belong." I liked how he could make me forget my step-mother. I smiled at his sincere humor. I needed more friends like Raj and Kiran.

❧

The weeks went by and I was confronted with new dresses, hairdos and shoes. My stepsisters seemed to enjoy modeling for me. My money, my house and they didn't stop to think I might resent it. I tried to ignore it all, but a small black pit formed in my stomach and I couldn't seem to fill it with happier things. I could forget my thoughtless family when I went to see Raj and Kiran, but I would eventually return to see my sisters all dolled up, practicing for the cotillion. As the dance neared, it only got worse. For the first time, I was truly happy I worked nights so I wasn't inundated all my waking hours.

"Two more weeks, Raj," I sighed as I sat down to watch him work, "I will be happy when this dance is over so I don't have to watch my sisters preening anymore."

"I've been thinking, Ella," Raj said quietly, "what if you paid for the charity tickets." He knew I didn't have that kind of money.

"Raj, I'm lucky to pay for the gas to get to work," I said. His smile was devious and he leaned closer.

"What if the company paid," Raj whispered, "it's your money anyway. Or it will be."

"You want me to embezzle?" I asked with a little shock.

"You would be stealing your own money," Raj justified, "my program will make it impossible to trace and you would be where you should be."

"There's not enough time," I wavered, "Agnus would see me there anyway and we would find ourselves in prison." The idea of attending the function did have a strong appeal. To see my sisters hopelessly flailing at men would be worth the entrance fee.

"Agnus only sees you as you are," Raj continued, "if you rid yourself of your ponytail and glasses, add some makeup and a new hairstyle, I would have trouble recognizing you." I shook my head.

"There's not enough time," I repeated. Raj smiled again.

"Kiran has a friend who is a seamstress. She does alterations for wealthy women," Raj argued, "you can borrow a dress for the night."

"Kiran is in on this?" I asked. Raj's smile was growing.

"She wants to see you all dressed up," Raj said, "she thinks you miss too much of life." I couldn't believe Kiran was in on the conspiracy. It made it seem more feasible.

"I can't see without my glasses," I conceded.

"Contacts."

"I can't afford contacts." I admitted. I would have to save up and a week wasn't enough time.

"Your company can." Raj was countering all my objections. "I can crack Coupon Crave's servers and get you in on a contacts deal as well as limo and hairdresser. I have to fit you in after the fact, but they will never know and I'll make sure you pay everyone." I stared at him. My friend was a master criminal and I never knew it.

"You owe yourself this," Raj continued, "you can't wait till you're thirty-two to start living. You'll get too used to being alone. Kiran and I don't want to see that."

"You sure we can't get caught?" I asked to reassure myself.

"It would take someone very skilled just to know they had been hacked," Raj replied, "even more talented to trace it back to the last proxy. No one has seen code like this before. They won't even know what they're looking at."

"It really is my money," I said, trying to convince myself. Raj looked pleased with himself. He knew he nearly had me over the edge and ready to say yes. "I would really enjoy watching Drizella and Anastasia bomb."

"And you might even meet someone," Raj added. In my dreams. Raj was already taken and everyone else works days. I questioned whether there was another vampire out there for me. A little flirting may not hurt, though.

"Kiran will help?" I had no idea while I kept piling requirements on. Raj just nodded. "Okay," I committed, "let's do it." Excitement replaced the black pit in my stomach. Raj turned to his terminal and went to work. He turned his chair around and handed me a phone.

"Type in a password, something unique," He said.

"Whose phone is this?" I asked, turning it over. It was just a slim black smartphone.

"Yours," Raj said, "present from Kiran and I. It's prepaid so it's not tied to your name." He always knew I was going to cave and say yes. I laughed softly. "Something somewhat long so that it can't be broken into. I have some encryption of my own invention running on it. Without cracking the password, it's contents are useless." I thought for a moment, then laughed to myself as I typed in the first memorable thing I could think of. It was fairly long but made me smile and I wouldn't forget it.

"What name do you want to use?" Raj asked as I handed the phone back to him. This was going to be completely cloak and dagger. I picked the first thing that came to mind.

"Cindy," I said, "Cindy Thompson." Raj began typing. He worked for over thirty minutes with joy in his eyes. He was impressing himself as much as he was impressing me. He went back to the phone and began working on it, then back to his terminal. Finally, he handed the phone back to me.

"All set Cindy," Raj said as proud as one man could be, "you have an appointment for tomorrow at the eye doctors, it and all the rest are in the Coupon Crave app on the phone. Your ticket for the charity ball is in the email account I created for you."

"You are incredible," I complimented.

"Just toss the phone away when you're done," Raj added, "it's the only thing that comes close to tying you to the fact you stole your own money." I had no choice, I hugged him. It made him uncomfortable, but I needed too. He was smiling when I separated, so no harm done.

~

Kiran helped me choose a dress. Had I seen it in a catalog, I would have never picked it out. When it was on my body, I couldn't not choose it. A soft champagne pink fabric that was cut and sewn in such a way, it looked like it came over my shoulders loose and wrapped my breasts, then tied off in the back. Below the faux wrap, a pleated high shirt started and flowed ever more sheer to the floor. It was soft elegance. Kiran's friend, Samantha, altered it to fit snug around my waist and drop into my cleavage. Just enough showing, to tease, but not arouse. I felt beautiful.

"Now, no stains or anything," Mary reminded me, "and take care to not snag it when you enter or leave the car." It made me a little nervous. I knew it was an expensive dress.

"I'll take good care of it," I replied. I could see her apprehension. She was doing this as a favor for Kiran and didn't know me at all.

"It does look good on you," Mary smiled. Kiran agreed. I twirled a couple of more times in front of the mirrors. It was the best I had ever looked.

"You need to stop in and see Madam Winslet," Mary continued, "she would have the perfect shoes for that dress. She owns a boutique off Harlem."

"Sounds expensive," I said.

"You have to have the right shoes," Mary instructed, "she's a friend of mine. I'll call ahead and make sure she gives you her best price."

Mary was right. Madam Winslet sold me a pair of pink heels that really completed the dress. I would be paying them off of the next six months, but I did get a 50% discount off the $1,500 list. They became the most expensive piece of clothing I had ever purchased. Most likely, I would wear them only once.

$\sim$

*I* slept in the control room, the night before the cotillion, under Raj's watchful eye. It wasn't comfortable and I was only able to grab a couple of hours, but I needed them for the day ahead. I would add a few more hours in the morning then off to the hairdresser. I had an 11:00 AM appointment. The Limo was supposed to pick me up at five. It would be tight, but the hairdresser was close to home and Kiran was there to carry me through the final stages.

The hairdressers accepted my phone's Coupon Crave coupon without question. I was a little hesitant when I handed it to them to verify, but Raj had done his job well.

"My name is Daphne and I will be taking care of you." The woman said as she approached. I smiled as the blonde led me to a chair. Her hair billowed out near her shoulders and seemed to frame her face well. I had high hopes for my hair as well. "Beatrice will join us in a moment to handle the makeup." Daphne smiled to set me at ease as I sat down. "Now what are your looking for, dear?"

"I'm not sure," I admitted.

"Something elegant," Kiran jumped in, "she's going to a formal ball."

"That will be fun," Daphne stated as she fluffed my hair,

"maybe a high braided bun with a few accents strands running loose. It would look divine with your skin tone." She tucked some of my hair up high on my head, "we'll have to add some high-lights to make it pop." The last time I had a high maintenance hairdo was when I went to prom. I would have to take her word for it.

"That sounds nice," I said, looking at Kiran for help.

"Lovely," Kiran agreed. I felt better about my decision.

"My head is yours, Daphne," I directed. She removed my glasses and started with a warm wash that felt so good I almost nodded off. My light brown hair was then professionally highlighted with soft dirty blonde streaks that seemed to blend perfectly, almost like they had been there all along. Daphne knew her job.

"Your first big dance?" Daphne asked. She was trimming away my split ends and cleaning up hair by my neck.

"Prom was the last one," I answered, trying not to move my head.

"We'll make you the star of the ball," Daphne smiled, "you'll have men throwing themselves at your feet." I tried not to laugh, not wanting to disturb her scissors.

"I'll just be happy to not trip on my own feet," I said with a smile in my eyes.

"Nonsense," she continued, "you have wonderful bone structure and with a smile like that, they will be fighting for a dance." I felt my face blush. I don't know how much I had embezzled for her services, but it wasn't near enough.

"It's been awhile," I joked, "not sure I remember what to do with a man."

"It's like riding a bike," Daphne quipped, "but a lot more smiling comes with the sweating." I couldn't stop the laughter this time. Kiran's face wasn't helping. "You'll have to be still if you don't want to look like Medusa." I settled down, struggling to hold my smile in check as Daphne went back to work.

Daphne pulled my hair into a tight braided bun with a few small trailers that were curled down the side of my face. It felt strange not to have a ponytail hanging behind me. My head felt freer with nothing to resist my neck from turning.

"Absolutely wonderful," a large woman said as she moved toward my chair.

"This is Beatrice," Daphne said, "she'll take care of your makeup." Beatrice walked around the chair looking at my face, her fingers drawing shapes in the air almost like she was finger painting.

"What color is the dress?" Beatrice asked.

"I have it in the car," Kiran announced.

"If you could bring it in, it would help," Beatrice added, not looking at Kiran. Kiran ran off quickly. "We don't want to do anything that would lessen the dress or the hair," Beatrice mumbled, "they should compliment, be friends and laugh together." I was a bit worried she might be insane. "I never try to build beauty, only bring it out. Gently steer the eyes in the proper direction, but never demand their attention."

"She's an artist," Daphne commented, "trust her and you will be pleased." I had little choice since I was already way out of my league. Kiran entered with the dress. Beatrice pulled back the plastic and held a small portion of the fabric under my chin. Her head moved wildly from side to side, then up and down. She was looking from every angle. She handed the dress to Kiran and wordlessly shooed her away.

Daphne brought over a large case and set in on the counter. The top opened down the center and it unfolded into numerous trays filled with all sorts of makeup products. Beatrice took one last look at my face, turned and grabbed a jar with acuity.

"Close your eyes, dear," Beatrice instructed. I did and relaxed as the chair lounged back. I heard a stool sliding up next to me. She went to work. She was humming some tune I almost recognized as she lightly applied something to my eyelids. Fingers, cloth, and brushes moved across my face with expertise. For all I knew, I would look like a clown, but she didn't seem to be making any deviations from her intended vision. She paused for a moment when I yawned. It was, after all, my internal clocks middle of the night. The work continued when my mouth settled.

I was almost to dreamland when Beatrice announced she was finished. I opened my eyes and saw three heads staring at me with smiles. Daphne raised my chair back into a sitting position and they all stepped aside. I could barely recognize the face in the mirror. Daphne's hair and Beatrice's face combined to give me sophistication with an air of fun. I smiled. The face in mirror glowed. I had never looked so good in my life.

"Camera?" I asked Kiran. She fished her phone out of her purse and captured my new look. It would only last for the night and I wanted proof.

"You're gorgeous," Kiran said as she examined the screen on her phone to make sure the picture came out. I turned to Daphne and Beatrice.

"Thank you," I gushed, "you're miracle workers."

"It's all in the raw materials, my dear," Daphne said, waving the compliment away.

"We did do good, though," Beatrice smiled as she nodded. I suddenly couldn't wait to get home and don the dress.

"4:15," Kiran announced, "we have to rush." I left a sizeable tip. I couldn't really afford it, but I haven't been this pleased with my looks since I figured out my parents were biased when I was five years old. I grabbed my glasses off the counter and headed out the door.

Kiran and I hurried to her house. I put in my contacts and stashed my glasses and a change of clothes in Kiran and Raj's guest room. When I came out of the room fully dressed, Raj gave me a wolf whistle. Kiran smiled and didn't even scold him. Aanya was wide-eyed, her expression said it all. I twirled, watching the hem of my skirt billow out. Everything was perfect. I had never been perfect before. Tonight, I would be a princess.

The doorbell rang. Our timing was perfect. Raj opened the door to two gentlemen in black chauffeur livery. "Elite Limousine at your service," the older of the two bowed. The younger, somewhere in his twenties was staring at me. He got an elbow from his elder. "I am Jaq, your driver," the elder smiled as he spoke, "and this is my son, Gus. He will be handling the doors."

"Pleased to meet you," I said and for the first time since a fifth grade play, I curtsied. It seemed so natural and the dress seemed to flow with it. Aanya giggled and I shared a smile with her.

"Are...are you ready, Ma'am?" Gus stuttered. His eyes were still taking me in. He made me feel even more beautiful. I smiled at him and his face went red. Yes, I was more than ready. Kiran giggled.

"I am ready, Sir," I said, moving toward the door. Kiran rushed forward with the small pink hand purse I had found at the store. The color was perfect for my dress and held my phone and some backup makeup. Everything else, I left with Kiran.

Gus held the door of the limo for me. He looked gallant doing it and had obviously been given instructions on how to stand. Jaq seemed proud of him. I thanked him as I entered which brought a smile to his face. There was room for ten people in the back of the limo. I was careful to tuck my dress carefully so it would keep its shape as I sat. Gus made sure my dress was completely inside before he closed the door and joined his father in the front seat.

"We should have you at The Fountains in twenty minutes, Ms. Thompson," Gus said and pushed a button which started a divider rising up behind the driver seat.

"Please," I said, startled at being closed in, "I would rather you didn't close me off."

"Of course, Ma'am," Jaq said with a smile and lowered the panel. He started the car and headed down the road. "It is a fine night for a dance," he commented, realizing I preferred conversation.

"I am so looking forward to it," I said with a formality that was born from the dress, "It has been a long time since I have attended one." I didn't tell them it was my high school prom.

"I think you will make quite the impression," Jaq continued, "Grace and beauty always play well at these affairs." I felt my cheeks warm. Grace and beauty.

"I borrowed the dress," I admitted, to embarrassed to accept all the credit.

"A shame you can't keep it," Jaq said, "you wear it so well."

"I...thank you," I said, unused to the compliments.

"It's really pretty," Jaq added. My smile was becoming permanent. Jaq was turning in his seat, I suspect to face me. A stern look from his father had him cease and return to facing front.

"I don't usually go to these types of things," I said, as I realized the ball was becoming a reality. A little apprehension was sneaking in.

"You will have no trouble fitting in," Jaq countered, "Though I suspect you will be exhausted from all the offers to dance."

"I am afraid I don't know anyone there," I admitted. I would know my step family, but I was intent on avoiding them.

"It's all in the advertising," Jaq said, "just say yes to the first dance request and make sure you're seen on the floor." He chuckled almost to himself, "The single men will go into combat mode to get the next dance. I must admit, I find you brave to attend unescorted." I wasn't sure if I wanted to cringe at the thought or bask in the glory of being brave. I looked out the window, now wondering if I had made the right decision. I did it more to have a secret fight with my step mother. A battle she wouldn't even know we were having.

"Gus and I will be right outside," Jaq continued. I think he sensed my apprehension, "If you need to take a breather, thwart a suitor or leave early, we are at your disposal." I smiled at him. I could use a couple of brothers for emotional support.

"That is good to know," I said, "I might take you up on that breather. Any other pointers?"

"Just smile," Jaq said. "It's usually pretty stuffy at these things and you are going to be like a fresh breeze." I blushed, happy I chose not to drive alone to the event. I needed my embezzled pseudo brothers.

I spent the rest of the trip learning about Jaq and his son. Gus was learning to take over his father's business and he made sure I knew he was currently unattached. I was flattered with his subtle flirting, knowing that his father would keep it in check. He was a nice guy, but not my kind of guy. I couldn't really define what I was looking for in a man. I only knew what wouldn't work. I wasn't even sure a perfect partner existed for me. Given my current work schedule, he would have to be part vampire.

Gus deftly pulled the limo around the main fountain missing the other vehicles by inches. The building was called 'The Fountains.' Though I had driven past the front gate before, I could never see over the hedge grove that bordered the property. It was luxurious. Three story high roman columns stood sentry along the long stone porch. To each side of the grand entry steps, lay expertly trimmed bushes that were dotted with red flowers. Light shone through the tall windows, driven by elegant chandeliers that I could just make out since the main floor was raised a good ten steps higher than the drive. Finely dressed people, mostly couples were climbing the steps and heading toward the entrance.

Jag moved quickly to open my door. He was smiling as I exited, happy that his father's eyes were finally pointed elsewhere. I straightened my dress as I stood and did a quick turn around. "How do I look?" I asked Jag.

"Beautiful, Ms. Thompson," Jaq replied, with a tinge of desire. More flirting. For his benefit and because I couldn't stop it, I smiled honestly. I saw his cheeks go red again. It was all the encouragement I needed. "We will be parked near the walkway," Jaq added, pointing off to the side where a brick walking path terminated.

"Thank you, Jaq," I replied. I took a deep breath, straightened my shoulders and started up the stairs.

There is something about walking into a new experience where past knowledge was useless and perceived scrutiny is high. It raises the heart rate and increases stupidity. My heart went into overdrive as I pulled my phone from my purse. It took three tries to type in the long password that I no longer thought humorous. A well-dressed doorman scanned the invite off the phone and waved me inside with a smile. I almost tripped over the threshold.

I bypassed the coat check table and walked slowly into the ball-room. I was a fish out of water. People were gathered in small groups around the rim of the dance floor. There were small waist high tables scattered about that most of the groups had gravitated to. Waiters and waitresses roamed taking orders and delivering drinks. I had thought myself lonely before. I was desolate now.

Standing in the entryway seemed conspicuous and the last thing I desired was to be seen as obviously lost. I fought off the idea of running back to the limo. I moved slowly into the room, fighting the fear I knew was irrational. I set a goal. Find the bathroom I would eventually need. It let me move with more of a purpose.

"What a lovely dress." The comment came as I passed one of the small occupied tables. I questioned whether it was directed to me and turned my head late in response.

"Truly lovely," A second speaker stated. She was a mature woman oozing sophistication. Her smile seemed honest though her posture was starched proper. Her friend, I suspected the initial speaker, stood a little more cavalier though her jewelry spoke of years of wealth. Both were in conservative, but appealing gowns.

"Thank you," I stammered. My feet stopped oddly out of sync with my turn. I was both happy that someone had spoken and nervous that I may enter into a conversation out of my league. The cavalier women smiled and covered a small chuckle with her hand.

"Stop it, Betty," Ms. Sophistication scolded, "she is nervous enough." She turned to me, gracing me with a warm smile. "You look like you may need a friend. Would you like to join us for awhile?" I had never heard kinder words in my life.

"Yes, very much," I said with more enthusiasm than appropriate. Betty's smile became inviting as she made room for me to slide up to the table. I saw they both had glasses of wine untouched in front of them. They may have just arrived.

"I am Ruth and this, of course, is Betty," Ms. Sophistication said, "and you are?"

"Cindy," I replied, happy that I had enough sense to not say Ella.

"I gather this is your first shindig," Betty said, ignoring the scowl on Ruth's face. Betty was a straight forward woman who didn't hide her intentions. She moved quickly to the point and wasn't overly concerned with niceties. I liked her.

"Yes," I said, more in my element with Betty, "this event is a lot nicer than I am used too."

"Well you certainly dressed for attention," Betty complimented. Another scowl from Ruth. "you'll have those boys eating out your hand." I suppressed a laugh.

"I'm not really here to find a man," I admitted, "it is more of a small revolt. I was told I couldn't go and I decided I could."

"Never let them tell you no," Betty insisted, jabbing her finger on the table to emphasize the point. "I like you already."

"But be pleasant when you do it," Ruth said softly, trying to counter Betty's aggressiveness.

"Would you like something to drink?" A waitress had snuck up behind me.

"Yes," I replied. At $5,000 a ticket, I should drink a few gallons. "some wine would be nice."

"Red or white?" The waitress queried. I had no idea how to answer. It depended upon how sweet the wine was. I was always partial to whatever was on sale and had a screw off top. I knew I was thinking too hard when Ruth jumped in.

"Why not try both," Ruth said, nodding to the waitress, "then you can decide your flavor for the night." I didn't even know that was an option. I looked up hopefully at the waitress, but she had already moved on, Ruth's suggestion taken as the order.

"Thank you," I said, smiling at her diplomacy.

"Excess is always the main theme at these things," Ruth instructed, "never fear to ask for what you want. It is expected."

"Ugh, those Tremaine girls are here," Betty said, her eyes pointing to the entrance. I took a quick look at my stepsisters and their mother. I had to admit they looked good. If they kept their mouths shut, they might attract a few men. "Those two have been hunting for gold the last four events," she continued. My face reddened. How much of my money were they using to fund their safaris?

"Hunting?" I asked, keeping my back to my sisters. I knew the answer, but I wanted to keep the conversation going. I enjoyed stepsister gossip.

"Husband hunting, my dear" Ruth replied quietly, "they aren't very good at it. Hard to get is not in their repertoire." I stifled a laugh. Betty didn't quiet hers.

"Sorry, Love," Betty apologized into Ruth's scowl, this time hiding her smile. I was surprised how she said it. It sounded like she meant it. "It's their mother that eggs them on," Betty continued in a whisper, "she was somewhat successful in her hunting," she shrugged her shoulders, "like mother like daughters." That was an astute observation. My stepmother was very successful. Too successful. Maybe I owed my stepsisters some slack. Like me, it's not their fault they were saddled with Agnus.

A waiter stopped by offering small plates with mixed hors d'oeuvres. Ruth accepted one for the table along with a set of cloth napkins. The waitress followed a moment later with my red and white wine. I sipped the red, cringed at the bitterness I wasn't expecting. The white was a lot sweeter with a nice fruity finish.

"Looks like the white appeals to you," Ruth said, smiling at my taste testing. I must have made quite a face when I tried the red.

"I guess my palette is uneducated," I said, trying to sound suave in my ignorance.

"Nonsense, " Betty said, "your tongue knows what it likes." I saw Ruth send a smile Betty's way. I began to notice they shared a lot of special looks. They must be friends from way back.

The snacks were to die for. All were finger food, the napkin your only plate. I watched Ruth bite into some kind of roll, holding the napkin daintily under her chin. I copied the movement when I bit into a cracker with some kind of seafood concoction. It melted in my mouth. A tangy mix with a hint of sweetness, crab I think, offering a soft texture against the cracker. The real problem with assortments of hors d'oeuvres, there isn't enough of the ones you really like. The seaweed and rice roll was pretty good, but the crab cracker was my favorite.

While we were sampling the food, Ruth and Betty were giving me an education about the families present. The Gildersons, old money made prior to the civil war in the slave trade. They gathered as a group after pushing three of the small tables together. The Wilkersons, newer money made by owning many local radio and television stations. They were a rather loud crew and seemed to be laughing more than talking. The list went on as I began to lose track of the names and occupations. Ruth and Betty were an encyclopedia of family knowledge.

"Excuse me, Miss," Betty said, waving down one of the roving waitresses.

"Yes, Ma'am."

"Those crab crackers, what are they called?" Betty asked.

"Crab on a Cracker, Ma'am," the waitress replied with a smile that wasn't insulting.

"Of course," Betty smiled back, "can we get a plate of those and another glass of white wine." Betty and Ruth were handling me. It was going to be a better evening than I thought. "and thank whoever is making the Crab on a Cracker."

"Yes, Ma'am," the waitress nodded before she headed off.

"Thank you," I said to Betty. Ruth beamed at Betty with pride. My mouth moved before my brain could stop it, "are...you two...a couple?" I wished I could take it back as soon as I said it. I was sure my cheeks were turning red.

"For thirty years, dear," Ruth said with a soft smile. I was so thankful I was right. Some might find the insinuation insulting. Ruth and Betty shared a look that only a couple would understand. I raised my almost empty glass.

"To thirty more years," I toasted. Ruth laughed and didn't scowl when Betty joined her. I was at the perfect no-pressure table. Our glasses clinked and we drank to their years. I was then treated to their history, difficult courtship, family trauma and finally the inevitable acceptance by all. It was a good tale that we were able to share many Crab on a Cracker over. More than once they had me laughing. The third glass of wine didn't hinder the amusements.

"Those are the Charmings, of the Boston Charmings," Ruth said, her eyes leading to the entryway, "Daniel and Rebecca. They are the ones who sponsored this ball. Lots of old money, railroads and stockyards." I looked over at the man and women who entered with strong smiles. Many of the guests turned and greeted them as they entered. They seemed comfortable with each other, every now and again they would find a reason to touch each other, be it hand to hand or hand to shoulder during a chuckle. "That's their son Peter." I nearly spilled my drink.

Peter was my flat-tire Peter. My-breasts-are-beautiful Peter. I felt my face flush as I turned away quickly. I couldn't possible face him. He had seen me practically naked and he knew me as Ella. I tried to suck my breasts into my chest. I downed the rest of my wine and took a deep breath. I wasn't sure I could stay knowing he might see me. Damn he looked good, somehow taller out of the rain.

Thankfully, the band started to warm up. The sounds distracted the ladies from my obvious surprise at seeing Peter. The warm up sounded like the band tended toward a brassy swing. I wasn't sure I could hold my own with that kind of dance. That and Peter, I was as uncomfortable as when I first entered.

"Cindy," Ruth said, waiting for my eyes to acknowledge her "you're looking a bit pale. Are you feeling okay?"

"Fine," I said, after letting out the breath I was holding. I forced a smile to my lips, trying desperately not to look back at Peter. I was waiting for the shout 'Hey, aren't you the naked tire girl.'

"We have to find you a first dance," Betty said, "someone polite who will keep his hands to himself." Sisters - that's how I saw Betty and Ruth. I never really thought of Anastasia and Drizella as sisters. We never really cared what happened to each other. Betty and Ruth seemed to have adopted me as their own.

"George would be happy to do it," Ruth said, "and a nicer guy you couldn't meet. He might spend a few minutes describing his stamp collection, but he'll move on if he sees your bored." Peter's hair looked softer now that it was dry. I glanced back briefly to verify. His eyes met mine. I snapped my head back. "What do you think, Cindy, do you want us to fix your first dance?" George wasn't Peter so it was better than embarrassment.

"Ahh, sure," I agreed, half-heartedly, "I'm not sure if I can dance well to swing."

"Just smile, Dear," Ruth chuckled, "men just want to think you're pleased with them." Ruth headed off, I assume to gather George.

"Peter Charming is not hard on the eyes," Betty said, her eyes alive with humor. She saw right through me.

"Who?" I stalled. I couldn't believe Betty was putting things together so quickly.

"Mr. tall, dark and dreamy," Betty said with a laugh, "the guy who has you all flustered."

"He doesn't know me," I said quickly. Too quickly. The ridiculous statement had a desperate tone to it.

"I could change that," Betty said, her smile turning evil mixed with teasing.

"Please don't," I begged. Betty lost her smile, examining my desperate expression. Her eyes softened and her shoulders relaxed.

"I'm only teasing," Betty said, her voice relaxed, "He's kind of a loner anyway." I knew she sensed my apprehension and was letting her kidding drift away.

"Loner?" I asked. Her statement surprised me. Loners don't pull off to the side of the road in a rainstorm and help people with their flat tires.

"He's some kind of computer genius," Betty informed me, "he isn't living off his trust fund like half the people here. Of course, building a personal fortune requires work and work requires time. From what I understand, he is married to it. Not that a lot of women haven't tried to change that."

"What's he doing here?" I asked.

"Hard to tell your mother no, I suppose," Betty chuckled, "she is still hopeful for grandchildren to spoil." I had to smile. My real mother, had she lived, would have wanted the same. My father would have been satisfied with happy and Agnus would prefer me out of the picture, something I meant to deny her.

"Here comes George," Betty said, pointing with her wine glass. I turned to find a well-dressed man approaching with a large smile. He was escorting Ruth, her arm entwined with his. His nose was speckled with prominent freckles that went well with his neatly cut red hair. More cute than handsome, his smile was welcoming. I found myself trying to copy it.

"Cindy Thompson, may I introduce George Gilder," Ruth said. George's eyes found mine, he held them with confidence.

"Ruth informs me you need a partner for the first dance," George said. His voice was unexpected. Deeper than his face advertised, more like a network anchorman. "I would be honored if you allowed me." Ruth was beaming. I assumed she had a special liking for George. I couldn't say no if I wanted to, and I didn't want to.

"That would be lovely," I replied, trying my best to assume the speech patterns from Downton Abbey. George's smile grew.

"How's the family, George?" Betty inquired in her trailer park way.

# HIS EYES TRAVELED FROM FACE TO FACE AS HE TALKED

"Wonderful, Betty," George said and moved himself to the table between us. His eyes traveled from face to face as he talked, seemingly including us all. "My sister had her baby. A girl she named Wilhelmina after our grandmother. So, I'm an uncle now." The conversation went deep into his family that Ruth and Betty seemed to know well. Normally, my mind would have drifted away, but George made it a point to include me and had me laughing at some of the histories. He was a charming guy.

"I think that's our cue," George said as the band started the first song. He held out his hand and I felt more than comfortable taking it. Luckily, it was a slower song, more big band than swing. The sax was nicely melodic. George led me to the floor, taking my right hand in his left and placing his right hand lightly around my waist.

"I have instructions to show you off," George said, "I am thinking I may just keep you for myself." I laughed at the humor in his eyes. "There's a lot of people wondering who you are."

"I'm nobody really," I said, my smile frozen to my lips. He spun me around so I was facing back the way we came. It was easy to follow his lead.

"Take a look at the girls," George said. I knew he meant Ruth and Betty. There was a small crowd around them. "See, your popularity grows. They're all wondering who the beautiful woman is." I looked back at George. He meant beautiful. My face heated up. "Blushing just makes it prettier," he added. His laugh was so forgiving I had to join him.

George was a wonderful dancer. He seemed to know when I might stumble and moved in a way to absorb the errors. He floated me around the floor as he pointed out people, warning me about some and complimenting others. His joke about my stepsisters was most amusing. We danced right by them and my stepmother without an inkling of recognition. Ella wasn't beautiful, but Cindy was.

"You're a wonderful dancer," I said as the song was winding down.

"All due to my mother," George said, "she insisted I take dance lessons for many years." He leaned in close to my ear, "I think she expected it would get her grandchildren quicker."

"How's that working for you?" I joked.

"My tastes don't lean toward women," George said, without a hint of it being uncomfortable.

"Ahh," I said, "and may I say we women are most disappointed." I came to fancy dance and the first three people I meet are gay. It was strange and somewhat comforting. No pressure to be anything but friendly.

"Thank you, Cindy," George said honestly. He spun me around, making my gown billow out in a most wonderful way. "I can see why Ruth likes you." The music stopped and so did we. After a brief applause, he escorted me, arm in arm, back to the ladies. The people surrounding them drifted off as we approached.

"Thank you, George," I said, my smiling emphasizing the point, "I really enjoyed the dance."

"As did I," George replied, "I need to make the rounds, but I would love a repeat sometime later tonight if I may."

"Absolutely," I agreed. I felt so pretty with him leading. I wanted to feel like that again. He nodded with his smile and excused himself.

"George is such a nice guy," I said to Ruth and Betty, "and what a dancer."

"He is perfect for a first dance," Ruth said, "a gentleman who knows how to make a woman look good." It wasn't hard to agree to that. I lost my smile when I saw Peter Charming from across the room. His eyes were on mine and he was walking toward the table. I looked away quickly, pretending I didn't notice, as embarrassment rose to the surface. I was sure he recognized me. I turned away, trying to find a place to move off to and avoid the confrontation. I rotated right into a sharply dressed man who begged my forgiveness even though it was I who bumped him.

"William Douglass," the man introduced himself with a smile, "I understand you are Cindy." Word was traveling fast. William had a set of bushy sideburns that reminded me of some of our ex-presidents from way back. Everything was neat and clean, but I had a strong desire to take a razor to those sideburns.

"Yes," I said smiling. anything was better than facing Peter, "it's very nice to meet you."

"Do you think I might have this dance?" William asked. It was a question, but the way he worded it I don't think he expected a no. With Peter on his way, it was as good an escape as any.

"I would be delighted," I replied. He held out his arm and I wrapped mine through it. Escorted, I moved to the dance floor and away from the impending embarrassment.

The tune was a bit livelier than when I danced with George. William kept it sensible, but did teach me a few spinning moves that were fun once I got the hang of it. He didn't have half of George's dancing skill, but he made up for it by ignoring my mistakes and laughing with me while I learned.

"I haven't seen you around before," William mentioned, his eyes were sparked with interest.

"This is my first one of these dances," I said, "I must say, I am enjoying myself."

"A lot of people see these things as some kind of requirement," William continued, "it's refreshing to meet someone who is here to have fun."

"What about you, William?" I asked, trying to get the conversation off me before he delved into my false identity, "fun or duty?"

"I thought it was duty," William smiled, "now it seems to have turned into fun." He spun me around again as I digested his veiled compliment. I was feeling pretty good about myself and he was feeding my ego even more. I was having a really good time.

"Something tells me you always have a good time," I bantered back. His confidence and smile defied his pretense of showing up being a duty. We did a couple movements that brought our opposing hips together which we executed rather smoothly. I was proud of myself.

"Maybe you can test your theory," William smiled, "Allow me to take you out to dinner next week." I must have looked prettier than I thought. It was a tempting offer, but Cindy wouldn't exist after tonight. How do you explain something like a name change? Not to mention, I was basically a janitor and he was obviously used to the finer things in life.

"You move quickly, Sir," I joked, not able to find a way to say no nicely.

"Too much pressure for a first dance?" William asked with a big smile.

"A little," I shrugged and promptly stumbled on the next step. He steadied me with a kind chuckle.

"I'll retract it then," William said, "but know that if we find ourselves at another function like this, I will make the offer again." I could hear the humor in his voice. He had expected me to decline his first offer. I instantly felt better.

"Next time," I said, "I might be inclined to accept." That seemed to please William and we finished the dance with good feelings. I needed to take a break. Sweating in my gown didn't really appeal to me. I was about to head back to Ruth and Betty when I saw them talking with Peter.

"William, can you show me the ladies room?" I asked. At least I could stall for a few minutes and hope Peter would move on.

"This way," William said, once again offering me his arm. He escorted me out of the main room into a hall, its sole purpose was to house the bathrooms. I thanked him kindly for the dance and we went our separate ways though I suspected I would run into him again that night.

The bathroom was huge. Along one wall, ten marble sinks, each with an individual oval mirror trimmed in some kind of gold leaf pattern. There were two attendants constantly wiping up water and handing out cloth towels. Each stall was as large as my utility room, complete with hangers, hooks, and a dark wood bench. I wasn't sure the need of a bench when the toilet was right there.

After struggling for a few moments, I found it easier to just remove my gown and then relieve myself of the night's wine. A heated toilet seat graced my bottom which made me smile. Such opulence. Even the toilet paper felt luxurious.

While a washed my hands, one of the attendants came over and straightened my gown and brushed off some lint I had gathered from somewhere. I wasn't totally comfortable with the attention, but I couldn't take it out on her.

"So, you're Cindy, the one that has everyone talking." I recognized the voice immediately. It was Anastasia and she was right behind me. I started washing my hands a second time, giving me an excuse to not look up. Peter outside, my stepsister inside. I shouldn't have come.

"I'm not sure I know what you mean," I said quietly, trying to slightly deepen my voice. I was going to work a few layers of skin off my hands at this rate.

"New people always generate buzz." It was Drizella. Great, both stepsisters. I grabbed a towel and started drying my hands.

"It is my first ball," I admitted then an idea struck, "Ouch," I groaned and squinted my right eye and brought the towel toward it, "I think something flew in my eye." The attendant rushed over to give me a hand as I turned around, my eyes squinting and the towel covering half my face. "You'll have to excuse me, ladies, it seems I can't see," I added for effect.

"Oh, how terrible," Drizella said, "of course." They both exited the bathroom quickly, not wanting to get involved in my problems. I knew them too well. The attendant, a young women with dark hair, smiled with me when they left. She realized what I had done. I handed her the towel and looked back at the mirror. I hadn't messed up the makeup on my eyes, which was good since I had left my purse on the table with Ruth and Betty. I couldn't hide in the bathroom forever, so I left after thanking the attendant who had helped me.

When I entered the main ballroom, I saw that my sisters had cornered Peter off to the right. His desperate eyes saw me just as I turned to the left. For once, my sisters would do me a favor as I moved quickly around the outside of the room until I ended up with Ruth and Betty.

"Poor Peter," Ruth said, "he is being waylaid by the Tremaines." I looked back across the room and watched his fake smiles and nodding as my sisters did all the talking. I felt a little pained for him, but not enough to ruin myself by rescuing him. I already had enough close calls and started to think I should call it a night. It had been fun and I enjoyed the dancing. I had never put Peter in the calculations when I thought of coming here. He could easily wreck everything.

"Are they really that bad?' I asked. Ella already knew the answer, but Cindy wasn't supposed to know.

"Think of leeches," Betty replied, "then give them barbed hooks and inane chatter." I covered my mouth when I laughed.

"Really, Betty," Ruth scowled. It was a wonder these two stayed together for so many years. They were so different. I did start to notice that Ruth's eyes sparkled when she scolded Betty. Maybe, Betty was Ruth's alter ego, saying the things that Ruth always wanted to say but was too polite to engage the words.

"He was asking after you," Betty commented.

"Who?"

"Peter Charming," Ruth continued, "he came by when you were dancing with William. He thanked us for coming as a pretense but then turned the conversation to you." I waited for the bomb to drop. I was sure he recognized me from the flat tire and told them I had another name. Ruth misconstrued my apprehension and smiled at me, "You shouldn't wear such a pretty dress if you don't want attention."

"What did you tell him?" I asked, realizing he hadn't blown my cover.

"The little that we know," Betty said, "we've been pretty popular since you've joined our table. A lot of people are trying to figure out who you are. I, for one, prefer the mystery. I think it makes you more attractive."

I panicked when I saw Peter had broken away from my sisters. He may not have figured out who I was yet, but if I gave him a closer look he might put two and two together. He was heading toward our table seemly ignoring the rest of the ball.

"I think I'll mingle," I said and quickly turned away from Peter and headed in the opposite direction. I had no idea how to mingle with wealthy people. I didn't have the social experiences necessary to draw upon so I walked aimlessly between the tables smiling, hoping someone would save me. Luckily, It didn't take long.

"Hello, Cindy is it?" A man said. Artist type with his brown hair pulled into a short ponytail. He was rather handsome, but I sensed he knew it.

"Yes," I replied, "and you are?"

"Rayburn Funderland," he returned, holding out his hand which I gracefully shook.

"Pleased to meet you, Rayburn," I said cheerfully, thankful for his rescue, "It seems everyone knows my name and I know so few."

"The curse of being new," Rayburn said, "and beautiful." His eyes twinkled when he added the last part. He had no fear and, I was sure, a lot of practice praising women. Normally I would back away, but it was either Rayburn or Peter. Rayburn, I understood. The band began a slow song. "Shall we?" Rayburn asked, his open hand leading off to the dance floor. I wanted to say no just because he was so confident I would say yes. It was the Peter effect that made me ignore my intuition.

"I would be delighted," I lied and he led me to the floor. I saw Peter out of the corner of my eye, grinning as he slowed once he realized where I was headed. I turned away, pretending I hadn't seen. I knew for sure now, he was hunting me. I couldn't run all night. I would have to plan an exit. If only Peter hadn't stopped to help me with my tire.

Rayburn was not a gentleman. George and William had spoiled me into thinking wealth brought with it a certain class. Rayburn was classless. He pulled me tight to his body, I retreated as best I could and spent the next few measures raising his hand from my ass to my waist where it belonged. I began to regret not choosing the shame that Peter would thrust upon me.

"We move together well," Rayburn whispered in my ear. The words slithered with sexual innuendo. I pulled back farther and again corrected his hand. His smile held confidence in my submission. I had lost my smile.

"You expect too much," I said clearly. I grabbed his wrist before his hand could drop back down to my butt. His grip on my other hand tightened.

"The fight is kind of cute," Rayburn said, "I like tigresses." He spun me in a circle and somehow ate up the space I created between us.

"Enough," I said firmly, but quietly. I didn't want to make a scene. I tried to break away from his grip but he tightened up and his confidence increased. I wasn't sure I could get away without making a scene.

"I think we both know where this is leading," Rayburn said, "why fight it. It'll be the most fun you ever had." I began to struggle and he just chuckled, tightening his grip and keeping me off balance with another spin. I got my knee ready. If you're going to make a scene, might as well make it a good one.

"No, Rayburn," I said clearly, knowing others would hear. Rayburn just chuckled and tightened his grip even more. He had been warned. It was the only warning I was going to give. I lined up my knee, aiming at his groin. It would ruin the dance, but I wasn't going to be treated like meat.

"I'm cutting in, Rayburn." Peter moved quickly, grabbing Rayburn's wrist. Rayburn released my hand. The two exchanged a look that wiped the grin off Rayburn's face. Rayburn's other hand released my waist and I let go of his wrist.

"I don't believe the lady agreed to dance with you," Rayburn growled. I thought there might be a fight in the middle of the dance floor. I saw it in Peter's eyes. He wasn't going to let go of Rayburn until Rayburn backed down. Rayburn wasn't going to back down.

"Thank you for a wonderful dance," I said sweetly to Rayburn, loud enough for close ears to hear, "I apologize for forgetting I had promised this dance to Peter." I gave Rayburn an out. He visibly relaxed, his fake honor intact. It was better than a knee to the groin. Of course, now I had to face Peter and all that came with it.

"Of course, Cindy," Rayburn said calmly, "women sometimes forget their commitments in my presence." It was all I could do not to drive my knee forward. He smiled for the crowd and headed off the dance floor. To my surprise, Peter filled the void *q*uickly, hand to hand, hand to waist, respectable distance apart.

"You picked a bad way to avoid me," Peter said, his smile eating past the lies I was trying to form.

"Avoid you?" I said, trying to give myself time to think.

"It's my duty to greet all the guests and thank them for their kind donation," Peter smirked, "you have been most troublesome to try and thank." I was sure I was turning ten shades of red. To make matters worse, Peter was a terrible dancer. Stiff as a board.

"You're a terrible dancer," I said, my smile growing. Work on his weakness and maybe he will forget the avoidance. Instead of losing his moral high ground, he laughed. His eyes crinkled, his lips curled and revealed a set of pearly whites that grew my smile all the more.

"I saved you from the hound and still you try and keep your distance," He said, "I've checked my deodorant twice, made sure I didn't have something in my teeth and ate a few mints. You're going to give me a complex." I didn't see any recognition in his eyes. Of course, I was practically naked and he was a man. Maybe he only saw my breasts. I softened my grip on his hand that had been tighter than necessary.

"You call Rayburn the hound?" I asked, trying to keep the discussion off me. His eyes were on me, though. They were intelligent eyes mixed with a bit of a whimsical boy. They only saw Cindy. I had been hiding for nothing.

"I could have warned you," Peter said, his feet moving like they weighed 100 pounds each, "had you not been disappearing every time I approached." That's why he was grinning when I accepted Rayburn's offer to dance. He knew I had worked myself into a corner. He just walked up and rescued me - no need to chase me down anymore.

"I thought all you guys were good dancers," I joked. I didn't want to explain my running from him.

"That's stereotyping," Peter countered with humor. He felt no shame in his inability to dance. "I was reading when these guys were in dance class." His eyes were still drinking me in. They shifted across my face and always returned back to my eyes. I moved closer, cutting the respectable distance in half. I liked Peter looking even if he couldn't dance.

"Do you read a lot?" I asked.

"All the time," Peter answered, his smile shifted to sly, "Do you run from your hosts a lot?" He wasn't letting me change the subject. There was a lot of intelligence behind those eyes.

"Do you chase down your guests a lot?" I riposted. His laugh brought mine to the surface. His laughter made the bad dancing enjoyable. I was surprised when he answered.

"I usually avoid the guests," Peter said seriously, "there is something about you that piqued my interest. I am not sure what it is, but I am going to try and find out."

"I thought you said it was your duty," I pointed out.

"So was going to dance class." This time, I started the laughter.

"There's a wonderful walking path around the grounds," Peter said when we caught our breath, "Would you like to get some air? I assure you I am highly skilled at walking." I wanted nothing more at the moment. I was kind of wishing all the people would disappear so we make each other laugh louder. I was so happy that he didn't remember Ella. He didn't even know he already liked my breasts.

"I'm not sure my shoes are fit for walking," I said. My heels would most likely fail on a stone path. At $750, I wasn't sure I wanted to try. Maybe I could go barefoot.

"The Fountains is prepared for that," Peter said with a smile, "they stock loaner tennis shoes just for these occasions.." He paused for a moment, "I assure you they are cleaned well between each use." I would have worn them dirty. I nodded in agreement, trying to shrink my smile. It was hopeless. I was going for a walk with tall, dark and dreamy.

We swung by Ruth and Betty who smiled knowingly as I grabbed by hand purse. It would have been rude to make them watch it if they intended to move on. Peter took my hand and led me out the main door, past my stepmother and stepsisters. I could see the envy on their faces. They forced smiles to nod at Peter. His speed increased as we passed them. I could almost feel his trepidation of possibly confronting them again. The silly warmth of revenge washed over me in a wave. They would never know, but I did. It was more satisfying than I would ever admit out loud.

It took about ten minutes for The Fountains to outfit me in a pair of pink Converse All-Stars. My gown made changing shoes difficult and I considered traveling back to the bathroom to get it done. Peter discounted the idea and dropped to his knees. His hands were wonderfully tender as he removed my heels and replaced them with the All-Stars. I never had a man dress me before. It felt warmly intimate even if it was only shoes.

"How's that," Peter said, rising to his feet. I took a few steps, assuring myself that everything was set properly for a walk.

"Perfect," I smiled. He held out his hand again. I took it as we headed out the door.

The walk meandered through the grounds. It was composed of tightly compacted brick in a fishbone pattern that would have easily eaten my heels. What we could see of the foliage in the darkening light was immaculately cared for. There were small ground lights, strategically placed behind foliage, that cast diffused light across the path. Just enough light so you could stay on the trail, but not enough to detract from the privacy.

"So," Peter started as we lost sight of the main doors, "am I ever going to find out why you were avoiding me?" I could make out his smile. He was enjoying his teasing.

"I never admitted I was," I countered. His hand squeezed mine. Shamefully, I squeezed his back. Cindy was such a tease.

"That means no," Peter laughed. He wasn't going to let me deny it. He was going to let it slide. "I interrogated half the room and found out almost nothing about you," he admitted, "Who is Cindy Thompson?"

"A girl on a walk with a guy," I answered. I didn't want to make up any more lies. The thought that it was Cindy meeting Peter hurt a little. It could go no farther than tonight.

"Your mystery is beguiling," Peter said, "I suspect there are things you don't want me to know right now." He paused for a moment as my mind reeled at his intellect. He was analyzing me, dissecting only the facts and assembling a picture that wasn't far from the truth. "I will let you have your secrets," he turned his head to me and smiled, "not that I have much of choice."

"You seem to like the mystery," I analyzed him, "why would I give it up?"

"I do love puzzles," he admitted, "they are so much fun to solve." We walked for a few steps in silence, still hand in hand. "Let's try a differ..." A buzzing in his pocket interrupted what he was about to say. I disliked the buzzing. "I'm sorry," he stumbled, letting go of my hand. I began to hate the buzzing. "It's rude, I know, but there are problems at work." He fished his phone out of his pocket. "It will only take a second."

"Charming," Peter cursed into the phone.

"What do you mean you can't?" Pause.

"Well trace the destination. You know what was exposed." Pause

"Let me know what you find." Pause.

"No, I'm not coming in." Peter disconnected without saying good-bye. He shrugged his shoulders with an apologetic smile. "Sorry." This time, I held out my hand. He took it. Apology accepted.

"Sounds serious," I said, "if they want you to come in."

"Actually," Peter said, "I am normally working at this time. The world is a lot quieter at night, makes it easier to develop," he chuckled to himself, "my mother says I'm half vampire." I started at his admission. He was on the same clock as I was.

"What do you do for work?" I asked. I already knew it had something to do with computers.

"Ahh," Peter laughed, "a puzzle for you. Revenge is best served quickly before it gets cold." I pulled him closer, my laughter merging with his. It was only fair. We walked around a bend that circled an old oak tree. There were a couple of memorial benches surrounded by flowers off in the corner by the stone fence. It was pretty in the dark, I thought it must be phenomenal in the daylight.

48

"Favorite movie?" I asked. If we weren't going to talk about our real life, might as well move to entertainment.

"That depends on my mood," Peter said, "right now, it would be Forrest Gump."

"You liked all the historical entanglements?" I asked, trying to keep the conversation on him.

"History was only the flavor," Peter said, he shifted his hand to encompass more of mine, "the story is all about how the geek gets the girl."

"But she died," I said sadly, remembering holding in tears the first time saw the movie.

"All that doesn't matter," Peter continued, "everyone wanted Jenny, but who did she marry and whose child did she raise? Who did she finally admit she loved?" I had always thought she had settled on Forest out of desperation. I had never looked at it from Peter's angle.

"I always thought Jenny was using Forrest," I admitted.

"She just didn't know she loved him yet," Peter smiled. He had an incorruptible view of the movie. He saw love where I saw capitulation. I liked his view better.

"All this time I thought she was a bitch," I laughed.

"Nope," Peter insisted, "Forest was just smarter. It took time for Jenny to catch up." I pulled Peter closer. His view was so much softer than mine. I imagined his view on real life was softer as well. I lost some of my harshness at that moment. Good riddance.

We spent some time talking about the books we've read and places we've gone. We danced around topics that could give away our pasts. It was a game and Peter was a master. He wanted something for everything he gave. For me, it was becoming inwardly painful. It was no game that Peter liked Cindy. It was no game that Ella liked Peter. I had created an impossible situation. How was I to know I would meet someone like Peter. Cindy would die tonight. Where did that leave Ella?

My phone buzzed in my purse. I pulled it out, flashing its soft pink cover as I quickly turned it to silent and put it back. I wasn't going to interrupt what little time I had.

"Even your phone matches," Peter observed, as he once again offered his hand.

"Pink is my color tonight," I said, "I am consistent, if nothing else." We rounded a small fountain ringed with little cement ducks.

"I like consistency," Peter said softly, no smile. He meant he liked me. Cindy did something stupid. Something Ella wouldn't do. She leaned forward and tilted her head up. Peter responded. His lips were a curse. A beautifully soft, caring curse. He couldn't dance, but he knew how to kiss. His hand found the back of my neck, cradling it in safety as my world became the two of us. The edge of excitement took over my body, cascading from my lips to my toes. I wrapped my arms around him and pulled him closer. I wanted so much more of him. I didn't want to share him with Cindy anymore.

"That...that was unexpectedly wonderful," Peter stuttered in my arms.

"You expected it to be bad?" I joked.

"I expected to take the rest of the night to work myself up to it," Peter said, "I liked it better this way."

"So you assumed I would just let you kiss me," I teased.

"No," Peter laughed, "I assumed I would work up the courage to try." His bravery wasn't in question as his lips took mine again. My hands combing into his hair as we tried to see how close our bodies could get to each other. I could feel how much he desired me. He was delicious.

"We should get back inside," Peter said after we had kissed forever. His face was a permanent smile. I was sure it matched mine. We were really good at kissing. I wondered if we were good at other things. Things that didn't require clothes.

His phone buzzed again. I began to really hate the thing. He apologized profusely as he answered it. I smiled and nodded as if it didn't matter. Life must have been easier before the birth of the mobile phone.

"Charming," pause.

"Well get a warrant." pause.

"That senator, what's his name, on the armed services committee," pause.

"Yep, that's him. He'll expedite it," pause.

"Call me when you know more." Peter ended the call with another apology to me.

"Sounds serious," I said as I returned my hand to his. He gave it a squeeze. I liked keeping the physical contact. It was a simple pleasure that seemed to affect my whole body.

"Someone is rattling my cage," Peter admitted, "it's time dependent or I would just turn off my phone. Sorry."

"You have senator's who do your bidding," I observed, "must be important."

"Actually, I do his," Peter laughed, "but if you find me more impressive the other way, I'll claim the power." We shared a smile as we continued our stroll back to the dance. Our hands swung together, our words easily finding things to agree on.

My mind was churning, trying to find a way to tell Peter about Ella. I didn't see a good way. Every way held shame and Peter's loss of faith. I couldn't handle him thinking less of me. I liked how Cindy looked in his eyes. I loved how he kissed Cindy.

I was about to remove my borrowed tennies when a cheer went up in the main hall. "The dancers must be here," Peter said. My confused look made him clarify. "Professionals. Come on," he said, holding out his hand. His excitement made me forget that I would be a few inches shorter without my heels. He led me quickly to a clear spot around the dance floor.

There were two couples, gymnasts by my calculations, throwing themselves around to a really wild Big Bad Voodoo Daddy song. The two girls spent almost as much time in the air as they did on the floor. Peter was enthralled, his hands clapping in rhythm with the crowd. I joined him as we traded looks, smiles, and a few hip bumps as the pros showed us all how poor of dancers we really were.

How they did it was a mystery. The four danced to two more wild songs, changing styles, but never tempo. I kept thinking one of the ladies would lose it and go flying into the crowd. It was an amazing feat of stamina as well as skill. The applause was deafening when the dancers finished the final dance. It was the first time I could tell they were breathing hard.

Without thinking, I put my fingers to my lips and whistled my appreciation. Heads turned, I flushed in embarrassment. The Fountains had never heard a whistle. On the other side, another whistle let loose. George, with a wicked smile, winked at me as he pulled his fingers from his lips. He felt no shame. I loved him like a brother at that moment. Protocol broke down as other whistles broke out and Peter wrapped his arm around me, laughing and pointing at George. I pulled Peter close, my shield against impropriety.

Peter's parents walked out to the center of the dance floor to congratulate the dancers. They made short statements, introducing the dancers and expounding on their exposition. Mrs. Charming then turned, looking directly at me, her smile was endearing. "It is no secret that my son spent his youth dodging lessons in the finer things of life," she paused as the audience laughed, "Tonight, he will pay the piper and please his mother by accepting a lesson from Mr. and Mrs. Longfellow." She indicated one of the pairs of dancers. I hid my smile as Peter vehemently shook his head, trying to wave off his mother with his hand. The crowd thought it a fine thing.

"I believe you have already selected your partner, Peter," Mrs. Charming said, waving us forward. Normally, I would shun the spot light. This time, I relished it. At least I knew he was a worse dancer than myself. I found his fear was selfishly making me bolder. I took Peter's hand and, to a chorus of laughter and cheers, pulled a hesitant man to the center of the floor. Mrs. Charming seemed especially pleased.

"If you leave me out here..." Peter whispered as we came forward.

"I'll never leave you," I said quickly. My heart thumped as the words left my mouth. They were Ella's words. They held more meaning than a dance lesson. I saw Peter's face go from grim to a silly boy grin. I was no longer pulling, he was coming of his own accord. He had felt the double meaning as well. He liked how it sounded. I liked how it sounded.

"Introduction?" Mrs. Charming asked Peter, her face almost laughing at his attention to me.

"Of course," Peters said, returning to protocol, "Mother, this is

Cindy Thompson. Cindy this is my mother, Rebecca Charming." Rebecca held her hand daintily. I tried to duplicate as best I could.

"So pleased to meet you, Cindy," Rebecca said with more friendliness than I expected.

"Very nice to meet you, Mrs. Charming."

"Rebecca, please," Rebecca said, "I'm so happy you have convinced Peter to allow me to tease him." Her face was lit up. She was enjoying herself. I can only assume that Peter had been more difficult in the past.

"It will be fun," I said, looking up at the smiling Peter. His eyes were boring into me, ignoring the surroundings. I quickly looked back to his mother. Her eyes were traveling between Peter and I at great speed. She seemed to see something that pleased her. I felt like a pawn between mother and son. Luckily, Mrs. Longfellow stepped forward to end the awkward confrontation. Rebecca relieved me of my purse so I had my hands free.

"Cindy, Peter," Mrs. Longfellow started, "we are just going to do a basic swing step." Rebecca stepped back out of the way, her smile still glued on her face. "face each other. Peter, lightly grasp Cindy's right hand in your left..." The instructions continued. We both heard and adhered to the lesson, but none of it was reaching long-term memory. It was if they were spoken from a distance, miles away. Peter's eyes and mine were making love with each other. Our feet moved as instructed, our bodies shifted and arms moved, but the eyes remained.

"I think you have it," Mrs. Longfellow announced. There was brief applause and well-meaning jeers from those who knew Peter well. We didn't care. It was all so far away. The music started and we kept dancing as others joined us on the floor. I don't think Peter realized he was actually dancing competently. I wasn't going to break the spell to tell him. It was all so lovely. Almost perfect. I only wished Cindy would leave. Ella wanted Peter to herself.

When the music stopped, Peter leaned down and kissed me. Not as one would kiss a friend, but a lingering, don't-ever-leave-me kiss. It was in the middle of the dance floor and completely inappropriate. It was a lovely thing and all mine. I wanted Cindy to die.

"Would you like a drink?" Peter asked, ending the kiss before I was ready. People were staring so I assume the kiss went longer than protocol prescribed.

"Water," I answered, my smile letting him know I wanted more of his lips. To hell with protocol.

"Ruth and Betty deserve some attention," Peter said, "I'll meet you there." He followed with a kiss that was all too short. I let him go, holding his hand until the distance forced it away. I stepped off the floor in a euphoria, thinking only of Peter.

"Your purse, dear," Rebecca surprised me, coming up from behind.

"Thank you," I said as I took it. Rebecca's smile was on the edge of comfort. She wasn't trying to disguise it.

"Peter seems to think a lot of you," Rebecca observed. I stopped and turned toward her.

"And I him," I said truthfully.The thought of my false identity flashed back at me. I had to tell him. I couldn't leave and not tell him.

"I don't think I have ever seen him...smitten," Rebecca laughed once she got the word out. I was a little uncomfortable talking with Peter's mother about Peter. I hadn't known him long enough to be allowed that type of comfort level.

"I am sure he is just being kind," I said.

"No," Rebecca continued, "smitten is the correct word." I feared her smile might crack her face. She reached out laid her hand on my arm. "I am just surprised is all. No one has ever gotten him on a dance floor and you have done it twice in one night."

"Surely..." I stumbled with a response.

"Believe me, he is smitten," Rebecca said, her eyes glanced over me, "and I, for one, am not disappointed." She smiled then added, "you have a wonderful night, Cindy." I think she sensed my comfort level had been reached. She had the same intelligence in her eyes that Peter had.

"You too," I stammered as Rebecca turned to walk away. I was relieved when she left. I was under enough pressure. I had no idea how to tell Peter about Ella. How would I ever tell his mother? I was screwing things up just by being here.

"Have fun outside?" Betty joked as I moved to their table. Her eyes were bouncing with inference to salacious ideas.

"Betty!" Ruth warned. Her scowl was forced. She was holding back a smile.

"We just went for a walk," I said, trying to keep everything G-rated, "we had a wonderful talk. He's a nice guy." Betty smirked under Ruth's glare.

"Peter seems *q*uite taken with you," Ruth observed, "I don't think I have ever seen him on the dance floor before." I smiled because I couldn't help myself. To think, I might be his first real dance. I knew I wasn't his first kiss. He kissed too well to be a beginner.

"It was fun. Did you see that he was actually getting good near the end?" I asked, trying to stick to facts and get the conversation away from the relationship.

"Everyone saw," Betty replied, "I think he would have jumped off a bridge if you asked." This time, Ruth didn't admonish Betty. She watched me, trying to see my reaction. I couldn't fight it.

"I like him," I admitted. Betty laughed and Ruth's smile went warm. Cindy was digging a hole too deep for Ella to climb out of. I needed to just fess up to Peter and let the chips fall where they may.

"That's a good thing," Ruth said, "I would hate to see that man's heart crushed." I wondered if that is exactly what I was about to do. Ella, the heartbreaker. I pulled out my phone, more to create space between the ladies and myself. I needed to think. Work out the words necessary to convince Peter this all wasn't some malicious hoax. I was sure it would involve a lot of apologies and groveling.

I turned it back on and keyed in my impossibly long password. I smiled as I typed. So very appropriate, even if Peter was unaware. A flood of texts and unanswered phone calls were listed on the main screen. Only Raj had the number. I checked the latest text.

Dump the phone. They are tracing it.

There were more of the same, mixed with apologies about Raj missing something technical. I felt blood rush in strange directions and my heart rate increased. I hadn't thought I might be caught. I was essentially using my own money. There was no way my stepmother could have found out, not this early. Coupon Crave wouldn't care if everyone was paid. Who were they?

I was about to head to the bathroom, maybe throw the phone in the garbage. I turned into Peter, smiling with a two glasses of water in his hands. "Your water ma'am," he said, making sure our hands met as I took it from him.

"Thank you," I replied, trying to hide my nervousness.

"You're looking rather please yourself," Betty commented to Peter.

"And why not?" Peter returned, "I have danced with a beautiful woman and just had the most pleasant phone call." His arm wrapped around my waist. It felt so right there. I needed to dump the phone, but I placed it on the table instead. My arm found comfort around his waist.

"Unknown relative leave you a fortune?" Betty prompted. I could tell she liked to get the whole story.

"Better," Peter said, "someone has been hacking my firewalls. Someone really good. It was only a fluke we noticed. We had experimental code running in front of the ticket site for this event to test it out. The same code we are planning to deploy for the military." Peter sounded excited, "Whoever it is hardly left a trace. It's only because we were running exhaustive post-tests that we saw anything at all." My heart was beating so fast. I was hoping Peter couldn't feel it.

"Your happy that you were hacked?" Ruth asked.

"Nope," Peter smiled, "I am happy that I may soon know who." He looked around the room. "We couldn't trace the source, but the destination of the purchases was traced to a single phone." He was almost giddy. I was sure I was pale as a ghost. "That phone is here. A team is coming with a handheld sensor to find the phone."

"How exciting," Betty commented. She was thrilled. I felt bile rising.

"Ladies and gentlemen," the band announcer spoke. All heads turned toward him. "grab your special someone and prepare for the midnight dance."

"I..I have to get my heels," I said, trying to smile through it all. Peter looked a little concerned. I assumed I sounded off. "I'll just be a moment," I added backing away from the table. He nodded and continued the conversation with Betty and Ruth. I turned and moved quickly. I was near the exit when I realized I left the phone on the table. My heart was trying to climb out my throat. I ran some words through my mind, reasons for going back for the phone.

Two men rushed past me. Cheap suits and even cheaper cologne. One had some kind of device in his hand, the other following. I watched it unfold in slow motion. I backed away slowly, closer to the exit as I saw my imagined future dash itself against the rocks. The men kept moving closer to Peter, I prayed they would turn. My eyes began to fill when the lead man pointed at my phone.

I couldn't stop the tears. The look on Peter's face went from disbelief to horror. He turned toward me, his whole face a distorted misery. I ran as the band started. There would be no midnight dance for Cindy. No life for Ella. I should have never come.

I ran down the main steps in my now stolen All-Stars. The crime wave continued. I wasn't sure how I got to the bottom safely with my eyes flooded with tears. Jaq had seen me coming and sensed the urgency. The limo was already running with Gus holding the door open. I still couldn't stop the tears. I had destroyed Peter and any chance I had with him. His face, the disappointment, was etched in my mind. He would never look at me again with those lovely eyes.

Jaq pulled the limo out smartly and waited until we were on the main road before he spoke. "Are you alright, Ms. Thompson?" I tried to answer through the sobs. My throat wouldn't allow anything coherent out. I just nodded and buried my face in the seat. Everything had fallen apart. The dream that was Peter was now a nightmare. I heard the divider slide up. Jaq knew when someone needed privacy.

The tears were under control by the time I returned to Raj's house. Gus opened the door and peeked inside as I was taking a deep breath. I let it out slowly, closed my eyes and did it again. My heart was slowing. I was wondering if I could be lucky enough to have it stop.

"You're home Ms. Thompson," Gus said quietly. None of the flirtiness he displayed earlier was there. It sounded more like he wanted me out. Of course, Cindy had run her course. Only Ella was left.

"Thank you, Gus, " I said as I exited.

"I'm sorry you had a bad time, Ms. Thompson," Gus said as he closed the door. From flirty to pity. A perfect end of the night. I heard the front door open and Raj came out of the house. There was panic in his eyes. Perfect.

Raj handed Gus some bills, a tip. I hadn't thought of that. "Thank you," Raj said as he shooed Gus and Jaq on their way. I felt like I was a lawn ornament. I stood there as Raj said my goodbyes and protected me from more pity comments. Raj didn't acknowledge me until the limo pulled away.

"I am so sorry," Raj said, "I missed the logs. I should have washed the logs." He was shaking his head.

"Doesn't matter," I whispered, "my shitty life returns. I didn't belong there anyway." I turned and walked toward the house. Raj followed with concern on his face. I was selfish and didn't accept his apology. I knew it was my own doing, my choice, but for some reason, I wanted others to suffer with me.

"Oh no," Kiran said when she saw my face. She had waited up as well. The tears returned when she wrapped her arms around me. I let her hold me. I held her back. Someone felt my pain and I let that comfort me.

"What happened?" Kiran asked quietly, once the tea was steeping. She had sent Raj away knowing I needed to talk.

"I found him," I choked. More tears.

"Who?"

"Him," I cried. Kiran wisely held me again. It took a few minutes for my control to return. Kiran was silent as she added sugar to the tea. She handed me a glass and we sat on the stools in the kitchen.

"Who is he?" Kiran asked. She took a sip of her tea, never letting her eyes drift from my swollen ones.

"Peter," I sighed, "he was the one." Her eyebrows raised. I took my own sip.

"Not the same Peter. Not flat tire Peter?"

I nodded my head. I let my eyes drop. "He didn't remember me, but it was him." I looked up, "I kissed him. He kissed me back. For a moment, everything was perfect and then..." This time, I held back the tears. I think my eyes were empty. "It was his computer stuff that Raj hacked," My head dropped again, "he knows it was me. The look on his face... I wanted to die." Kiran's hand covered mine.

"What if you talk to him?" Kiran asked, "it's not like you meant to hurt anyone."

"You didn't see his face," I said. The kitchen floor tiles held my attention. "I lied to him all night. He kissed Cindy, but he hates Ella."

"Was it a good kiss?" Kiran smiled softly as she asked.

"More wonderful than I had ever known," I admitted, "I didn't want it to stop." I looked at Kiran and let the truth go, "Had we been somewhere private, I wouldn't have stopped." I shook my head, trying to not dwell on the impossible. "It's all ruined now. He'll never kiss me again. Not the girl who tricked him."

"Men don't always think with their minds," Kiran whispered, "maybe he liked the kiss as well. Maybe he'll overlook a few bumps in the road."

"Bumps? You mean prison," I said, "he was way to excited to catch the person who hacked him. He took it personally. No... Cindy is on his shit list and Ella can never show her face."

"I'm so sorry, Ella," Kiran said, "I never thought anything bad would come of this. We just wanted you to get out there. You're too sweet to be by yourself."

"You didn't leave anything?" Raj asked, coming in without me hearing, "no one knows who you are?" His voice was shaking a little. His words lacking confidence.

"The phone," I replied.

"They won't be able to break the encryption," Raj was thinking as he spoke, his eyes looking out the window, "at least not in a timely manner. Maybe years at the earliest." He paced over toward the refrigerator. "You used a long password, right?"

"Yes," I said. It was humorous when I typed it in, but now it hurt to think on it. Raj's concern was evident in his tone.

"Raj, this won't get back to her, right?" Kiran asked, "I mean, everyone got paid. No one was hurt. Certainly they won't pursue it."

"It was a Shark firewall," Raj answered. He was ringing his hands. "the same ones the military uses." His face held a little panic. "I didn't think they would ever find out."

"You mean they will look for her?" Kiran asked.

"Maybe...yes...I think they might," Raj admitted, "they will look for her and me." Kiran's hand covered her mouth as her eyes widened. They both shared worried looks at each other. If they found Raj, they would deport the family. Their worries far exceeded mine.

"I won't say a thing," I said *q*uickly, "If this falls apart, I'm in trouble whether or not they know about you. No one ever mentions this again."

"It was all my idea," Raj countered, "I can't let you do that."

"You can," I demanded, "and you will. I will not have your whole family be torn apart because I was pissed at my sisters. This will end with me." It felt better to stop feeling sorry for myself. Proclaiming self-sacrifice was better than crying. "I was complicit anyway."

"But..."

"Kiran, your family comes first," I interrupted. Kiran wrapped her arms around me. A mother knew what had to be done. A stubborn husband would have to swallow some pride. They had Aanya to think about.

"Thank you," Kiran whispered in my ear. If it came to prison, at least I would have an endless supply of those potato things.

"My shoes!" I shouted, "I left my shoes." I pushed the All-Stars out from under my dress. Ella bought the shoes.

~

*M*onday night I was back to my fate. Seven more years of emptying trash cans and mopping floors. The difference was that I had a vision of what life could be. Struggle as I might, the kisses I shared with Peter refused to leave my mind. I cleaned harder and it was still there. I created my own world, earbuds blasting music as I mopped. All I could think of was a lousy dancer who kissed like a prince. The cotillion was a wish that would never come true.

I moved to the next office. Agnus' garbage was always filled to overflowing. Scraps surrounding the can, no effort to tamp it down and save me the tedium of picking up after her. A little more well-disguised torture. Down on my knees, I scraped up some sticky gunk that adhered scraps of paper to the floor. I swallowed hard and tried to not break down again. I had promised myself I would let it go. No more fretting over what can't be changed. At least the police didn't seem to be knocking on my door.

I wiped the sweat off my forehead and stood once the floor was un-gunked. I switched my music to something slow and tender. I had to be nicer to myself if I was going to last seven years. I took a deep breath and mopped Agnus' office as if it was my own. I danced with the mop. Peter was about as good.

I pushed the bucket out the door with my foot and finished mopping by the door. Agnus wouldn't notice, but I felt a brief sense of completion as I closed the door on a clean office. At least I had small victories. I pushed my glasses back up my nose and brushed some hair, that broke loose from my ponytail, back behind my ear. I turned toward the next office. Rebecca Charming was standing there, two champagne pink Madam Winslet pumps in her hand.

"Cindy? Ella?," Rebecca asked, "what should I call you?" Her expression was blank. In her case, I believed that meant anger. The mop and bucket were both a shield and the most embarrassing things I had ever held.

"I...I'm sorry." It stumbled out as I removed my ear buds. Had I an hour to think of what to say, it would have come out the same. Rebbecca just stared at me. The mop handle shifted to cross in front of my body. It was a weaker shield than I thought. "Ella," I answered before I had to move my eyes from hers. The bucket was suddenly interesting as I tried to dam my tear ducts.

"Peter is livid," Rebecca said, "he doesn't get angry. He broods, pouts and goes silent, but never angry. Somehow, you have done what no one has done before. You have made him irrational." I could see her head dipping low, trying to find my eyes. Damn tears. "Was that your goal? To ruin him." I turned away, letting the mop handle drop from my hands to the floor. I tried to get my mouth to form words. I took a deep breath, louder than I intended.

"Ah," Rebecca said, "can't face what you've done. You're awfully weak for someone who plays so harshly with other people." A small bit of anger flared. My stupidity was clear. Never had my intent be to hurt anyone. I turned on her.

"I didn't mean for any of it to happen," I said, louder than I should have, "it was a stupid idea. I didn't know I would meet Peter. I didn't know I would..." I stopped myself, trying to let the unwarranted anger dissipate. Peter's mother stood before me with a half smile I didn't understand. "I'm sorry it turned out the way it did," I repeated, softer.

"So, you're not an actress hired to prove him a fool?" Rebecca asked. The thought that Peter might think the kiss a fake hit me harder than I would ever expect.

"Oh, God!" I said, covering my mouth. I no longer controlled my emotions. The entire night flashed by again. His face when he realized whose phone it was. I collapsed against the wall. He wasn't disappointed. He hated me. My ass found the floor, my hand covered my eyes.

"I thought not," Rebecca said warmer than I deserved. She sat down on the floor next to me. "Luckily, the men didn't recognize the heels. Dorothy Winslet has been a friend of mine for many years. Don't hold it against her. She thinks she was doing you a favor by giving me your name." Rebecca paused for a moment. "You have some time, but my son is very determined," she paused for a moment, "as is the military."

"I'm in trouble," I said, looking up. I was sure my face was a mess.

"Yes you are," Rebecca said, her hand compassionately covering my arm. "How do you feel about my son?" Her question was unexpected. My words caught, but I knew I couldn't lie.

"Hurting him...I would have rather died," I replied, "I couldn't stop it." I shook my head, "I was going to tell him, but it just kept accelerating. How do you stop an avalanche." I looked at compassionate eyes that I didn't expect. "I ran."

"That's not an answer."

"What do you want me to say?" I said, my eyes streaming, "I'm a damned janitor and he's a..a..businessman," I didn't know what he was. I just knew it was beyond my dreams.

"Again, you're not answering."

"He's everything," I yelled at her, "proof that I can fuck up anything." My uncontrolled blubbering got worse as my eyes found the floor again, "I fuck up everything," I repeated quietly to the tiles. Every mistake I ever made invaded my mind and overshadowed the few successes. At that moment, I was a complete failure.

"Well," Rebecca said, "that's closer to an answer." I turned to look at Rebecca. She was smiling, soft and forgiving, and sitting next to me on the floor. Next to a mop and bucket. This woman was the definition of high society, but she was down at my level.

"You don't hate me," I observed. Her soft laugh filled the empty hall. I was missing something.

"You had my son on the dance floor. Twice," Rebecca explained, "he wanted to be there with you. You have no idea what that means, do you?" I shook my head. "He always hated dancing. Felt it made him look like an idiot."

"He's not very good," I added. Then again, either was I. Comparing him to George and wasn't really fair.

"No. No he's not," Rebecca continued with a small chuckle, "but that didn't stop him. He would have spent the whole night there if you had asked." I must have looked dumbfounded. "I have never seen him so...so...alive." She struggled for the word.

"Alive?"

"Happy," Rebecca corrected, "he didn't care if he looked like an idiot." Her eyes sought out mine," he only cared that you were there with him."

"Now, I suppose, he wants me in prison."

"If you heard him rant," Rebecca smiled, "prison would be too lenient. I believe I left when he was discussing the finer points of burning at the stake."

"Why are you here then?" I asked. I should have asked why the police weren't here though I didn't want to give her any ideas.

"I want to see him dance again," Rebecca replied softly.

"Is that before or after he burns me at the stake?" Rebecca's laugh echoed down the empty hall. At least the tears stopped, but it was too hard to join the humor I barely understood.

"Will you meet with him, Ella?" Rebecca asked, then she quickly added, "before this mess catches up to you."

"He would meet with me?"

"No," Rebecca smiled, "but he could run into you." I felt my stomach churn at the idea. I couldn't look into his eyes and see hatred. I remembered the butterflies when I first entered the dance. An arranged meeting would be a hundred times worse.

"I couldn't...to trick him again," I said shaking my head, "I don't want...I can't do it again."

"Please, think about it," Rebecca said as she stood and brushed off her pants. She held out her hand. I took it and she helped me to my feet.

"It would only make matters worse," I stated clearly, "I'm not built to hurt people." Rebecca gave me her smile again. It was too confusing speaking to her about Peter. She had some vision in her mind about a reconciliation. I had hurt him too much for that. I hurt myself too much.

"You work nights," Rebecca stated, looking around the offices for the first time. She was looking to change the subject. I was going to let her.

"Until six," I added. She handed me my pink heels. They might look nice with this year's prison attire. "Thank you."

"Think about, dear," Rebecca said as she started retreating to the elevators. I lied by nodding my head. "Oh, I almost forgot. Peter somehow knew your first name and that you drive a beige Toyota." I was sure my face went bright red, "He said something about you setting him up good."

"Shit." It came out of my mouth before I could stop it. He had remembered the flat tire all along.

"You should really work on your language, dear," Rebecca said, as she turned to the elevators, "Both you and Peter sound so uncivilized these days."

∼

"She was here?" Raj asked with panic in his voice.

"Yes," I said, "I think she saw Peter and I riding into the sunset together."

"If she could find you..." I nodded as Raj spoke. "I am so sorry Ella."

"It's my fault as well Raj." I shrugged my shoulders, "it's a first offense and all, I am hoping that it won't go far. I'm really hoping I don't have to face Peter again."

"I can't let you take the blame," Raj insisted, "It was my stupid idea, my ego that got you here."

"Nope," I said shaking my head, "If it was just you, maybe, but we have to think of Kiran and Aanya. Nobody is waiting for me to come home. They can't deport me. I'll probably get probation and have to stay away from computers." At least that was my hope.

I spent the last two hours of my shift deflecting Raj's apologies. We shifted a lot of the blame on Agnus since she was the reason it all started. It helped a little, but telling a judge that your stepmother is a bitch probably wouldn't help with reality.

I took stock of myself in those two hours. Raj and Kiran were my only good friends. My other friends had drifted away over the years. They slept nights and worked during the days. Our schedules prohibited anything meaningful. I was basically a janitor, stashed away to keep me out of my own business. I had let it happen. I'm not sure if there was anything I could have done, but I hadn't put up much of a fight. Agnus held the puppet strings and I never tried to cut them. I had a lawyer, young though he was, who said I was at her mercy. She was the executor until I was thirty-two and there was nothing I could do about it. I wondered if I had given in too quickly. It mattered little now.

Peter was on my mind as I was riding the elevator down. For a brief moment at the cotillion, I felt our shared desire. I wondered if there was only one person on the planet for me. If so, I was in trouble since I just kicked my one and only in the nuts. I tried to get that last image of him out of my mind. That look I had thought was misery, was most likely the beginning of hatred. I really wasn't any good at hurting people. It hurt me more.

I exited the building, thankful that Agnus decided to not do one of her early morning inspections. I had to take the good where I could find it. I fumbled for my keys in my purse and accidentally ran into someone outside the door.

"Excuse..." Peter's eyes met mine. I started backing away as I saw the recognition in his eyes. The building stopped my retreat. I watched as his face went through a hundred emotions, some of them frightening. He tried to speak. I tried to speak. I had no words. Sorry was too feeble. His shoulders lost their strength.

"You left me," Peter finally said. It wasn't an accusation. There was a tremendous amount of sorrow in the statement. My damn eyes were welling up.

"Do you hate me?" I asked. I didn't know what to do with my arms. They were moving like they were lost. Peter looked away, then back again.

"I can't," Peter admitted, "you're too close."

"I never..." I stumbled over my words, "I didn't mean...I didn't want to leave you." He moved toward me, his eyes as cloudy as mine. I leaned into him, risking everything. His arms wrapped around me so carefully, I knew I risked nothing. I tilted my head upwards and the most wonderful lips met mine. This time, it was he who led the dance.

"My mother set me up," Peter said, his smile defying his tone. I pulled him closer, not wanting to let him go.

"I told her not too," I whispered. How wrong I was.

"I suspect you are to join me for breakfast instead of her," Peter said, pointing to the 24-hour diner next to my building. "She spoke with you?"

"Last night," I replied, "don't be mad at her." Our lips joined again. Soft, forgiving and so filled with desire. I could feel my heart speeding. No, Rebecca had little to fear of retaliation from her son.

"You work nights?"

"Vampire," I nodded. I loved his smile. It was if the hacking incident never happened. All of the problems of the world disappeared and it was just to the two of us necking in the street at six in the morning.

"Breakfast?" Peter offered, his hand caressing the small of my back. I was leaning into him, liking the way his body felt against mine.

"I would love breakfast," I replied. I didn't want to lose contact with Peter, but we couldn't stay on the street like love-starved teenagers. We were love starved adults after all. He took my hand, obviously desiring the contact as well. I walked as close to him as I could without tangling our feet.

"I hate it when I have to admit my mother is right," Peter said, "she has this I-told-you-so expression that gnaws at me." I bounced my shoulder into his as we walked. "Don't snap to judgment Peter, you have to hear her side Peter, now you're just being irrational Peter." Peter's imitation of his mother's voice was way off. It made it all the more comical.

"I like her."

"I love her," Peter said smiling, "It's just that I sometimes I feel ten years old when I'm with her." He stopped walking and turned to me. "She was right, though. I don't care about the hows and whys. I just want to be near you."

"Even if my stupidity lands me in prison?" Peter's hand moved to the side of my face. I leaned into it, loving the way it felt against my skin.

"Even if," Peter promised. The street once again was treated to two people who couldn't keep their hands and lips off each other. I felt my pulse quickening as I let my passion loose. Our kiss became deeper, tongues dancing to our heartbeats. I was no longer hungry for food.

"I want to be with you," I said. The meaning coming from deep inside. A place that had been quiet for far too long.

"I would love to skip breakfast with you," Peter whispered, his fingers playing with my hair. I smiled at his agreement, taking his hand in mine. "I'm parked a block over," he said, pointing to the south. I had no apprehension. I led him down the street as a comfortable joy warmed me. I knew practically nothing about Peter, but I felt I knew him better than anyone else in the world. We were in some sort of sync. We knew we wanted each other and there was no wall of proprietary blocking the way. The excitement in his eyes fueled mine. Everything was exactly as it should be. Perfect.

"I have a million questions," Peter said, "but only one seems important right now. I don't know whether to call you Cindy or Ella."

"Ella," I replied, "Cindy was just for the cotillion."

"Ella...Ella," Peter tried it out for size, "Hello, my name is Peter and this is my girlfriend Ella."

"Girlfriend?" I said smiling. I knew I was. The kisses told me so.

"Why yes," Peter joked, "but you need to give me some time to break it to Cindy." It was tough to kiss him while I was laughing, but I managed.

The ride to Peter's condo was no different than our walk around The Fountains. We laughed and spoke freely about unimportant things. In silent agreement, we both ignored the outstanding issues. That was talk for later.

I walked into Peter's apartment expecting a dark bachelor pad. Instead, the morning sun was filling the open floor plan through tinted windows. A vista of Lake Michigan to the east, thin curtains blocking out the Chicago skyline to the south. I had never been in a Lake Shore Drive condo, much less a corner unit with a spectacular view.

"It's beautiful," I said with a little awe in my voice. I moved toward the window. The twenty-second floor hid the grime of the city below. It didn't hurt that it was a clear day.

"It certainly is," Peter said. I turned. He had been staring at me when he said it. I loved the look in his eyes. The idea that he felt the same way that I did was intoxicating. What little hesitancy I had, fled at the sight of his smile. For once in my life, I had no fear. I reached up and began unbuttoning my blouse.

Peter looked off toward what might be the bedroom door, then back at me. He was going to say something when I reached the last button of my blouse, revealing a rather boring white work bra. I raised the blouse over my shoulders and let it drop to the floor. His mouth began to move again, his eyes glued to my chest, nothing came out. I reached behind my back, unhooking the bra and unceremoniously let it drop to the floor. 'This is me, the normal me, in the bright light, take me or leave me,' I thought boldly.

# I NEVER FELT SEXIER IN MY LIFE

Peter's eyes took me in. I saw something click behind his eyes, triggering his smile loaded with desire. I had just left work, probably a mess, and I never felt sexier in my life. Peter moved toward me, lifting his shirt off over his head. On his trim waist, just above that pants line, there was an adorable small tattoo of a purple flower bloom. I tried to pretend not to notice, but a giggle escaped from my lips. Peter looked down at his flower, his smile deepening.

"Lost a bet," Peter said, "I have a sordid past." I reached down and ran my fingers along the purple ink. His stomach reacted in a ticklish manner. I could see the shadow of another reaction between his legs.

"Any other secret art?" I asked, my lips moving toward his.

"Nope."

"Damn," I said, just before my mouth found his. I pushed my breasts into his chest, enjoying his skin. Peter's hand ran up my waist to cup the side of my breast. Tingles ignited wherever his fingers traveled. Our tongue entwined as we explored. I could feel his heart beating as it fought to be louder than mine. Impatience got the better of me. I reached between us and began undoing his belt.

Peter's hand left my breast and moved to my pants. We separated slightly, trying to remain kissing as we raced to get the other out of their pants. Kissing turned to laughter as we fumbled to undress each other. Everything was backward and neither of us was particularly deft at the task. Neither of us was going to give up either. I was slightly disappointed when Peter claimed victory by sliding my pants down my hips.

Dropping to one knee, Peter lowered my pants toward my ankles. I lifted up my foot and he removed my shoe and sock. He repeated the process with my other foot. I stepped out of my pants and stood before him in only a conservative white panties. He reached up and sank his fingers in the elastic and slowly removed my last bit of clothing.

I had no idea why I wasn't running to hide. There was something about Peter that I trusted beyond good sense. I had never braved the light with any man before. With him, it felt like a requirement. A level of trust given. Trust that his eyes told me was well received.

Peter ran his hands up the back of my legs sending wonderful shivers through my body. His fingers teased along my backside as he leaned forward and kissed the top of my mound. His lips left wet trails has he kissed his way up my body, stalling on my breasts as he slowly stood.

"Absolutely beautiful," he whispered. I combed my fingers into his hair, pulling his lips to mine. I loved how his hands explored, sending pleasant waves across my skin. I have hidden nothing, me at my worst and he wanted more. I tried to get closer, climb into his skin. I no longer wanted to just touch. I wanted to join completely.

My hands moved quickly, finishing what they started with his pants. I felt animalistic, tugging anxiously, lowering his pants and briefs together. I paused when I felt his arousal. I was rather pleased my body had that quick of an effect on him. I turned him and pushed gently. His feet tangled in his pants and he fell back onto the couch. We laughed as I struggled to de-shoe and de-pants him.

Peter tried to rise when he was fully naked. I gently put my hand on his chest and held him down. Well, in truth, he let me. I slowly climbed up his body, my lips caressing what they found. His erection jerked when I gave it some attention. His desire. like mine, was wound tight and I heard him gasp. I rose higher, smiling at how excited he was. He looked so delicious as he reached out to help me up.

"You want to lead?" Peter asked. His smile told me he would be happy either way. I nodded as I dragged my breasts along his chest, our lips meeting again. I did want to lead. I had felt so out of control for so long, the idea of controlling things, however briefly, was exciting. I felt him shudder and knew he didn't mind at all.

I straddled Peter's waist, never breaking our kiss. He helped me, guiding my hips with his hands. I reached between us, grasping his manhood and lowered myself. Foreplay was for next time. Neither of us had the patience or the need. I separated from his lips and watched his eyes as we joined. We exhaled simultaneously as we became one. The glorious sensation of completion made my stomach curl and Peter moan. It was deeper than my past experiences. Meaning, I wasn't prepared for, emerged. I saw Peter's eyes water. I stopped when he was fully in me and stared in awe at how it felt.

"You're perfect," Peter said. He was so wrong.

"We're perfect," I corrected. Alone I was a mess.

"We," he whispered. Drawing our lips together again. Every movement became a new sensual experience. A hand down my side, my hand in his hair. I didn't matter how trivial, every touch ignited a new flame. I began to move my hips, desiring the wonderful internal friction that sent pleasure through us both. His hips joined mine though the leverage was all mine. I wanted it to last forever, but my body wanted more. A tingling began, his eyes, the way he looked through me, the heavenly feeling between my legs, traveling deeper than I thought possible.

"Let go," Peter said, sensing my need, "my love." His words, the sunrise over the water, the perfect us. My insides blossomed. Pleasure surged, following my bones to my extremities and I began to shake uncontrollably. Peter held me as his legs stiffened. His eyes found mine was we lost ourselves together. I collapsed into him, my muscles becoming happy rubber. I could feel him twitching inside of me, his breathing heavy with his release. We were perfect.

"My love," I whispered into Peter's ear. I kissed the lobe and felt his chest rise and fall in a chuckle.

"I meant it," Peter returned. I bit his ear with my lips and felt him tremble. I liked the reaction it generated.

"So did I," I whispered. Peter held me tighter. We stayed that way for a long while, enjoying the comfort of being as close as we could get. I learned how his heart beat in those minutes. Two quick beats followed by a pause. Slowly it degenerated to single steady beats. Each time it beat, I knew it was for me. It had to be. My heart was beating for him.

~

*I* remembered a bigger shower in high school, but it was built for entire PE classes. Peter's was the largest I had been in since then. It had a digital thermometer to set water temperature, a long bench along one side and many nozzles that shoot water in all directions.

"It came with the condo," Peter said as we stepped in. He set the temperature and pushed the on-button. It took a few seconds before the water began. "It doesn't start until the water is at the desired temperature."

"Such luxury," I complimented.

"You'll love this," Peter said, pushing a few more buttons. A large, overhead shower head began to gently sprinkle water. He took my hand and pulled me under the warm rain that seemed to be everywhere. It was a soft summer shower and we were naked in it. Kissing in the rain was a beautiful thing.

We spent a long time in the shower. Our after play more than made up for the lack of foreplay. It was if we had always known each other. I loved how he washed me in such a cherishing way. The way he would make me moan when his hands found my more intimate areas. The way I could make him squirm with my own fondling. The laughter that ensued from jokes only we could appreciate. It was by far, the most enjoyable shower I ever had.

Peter's phone rang while we were in bed. I was snuggled into him, enjoying the comfortable pillow he had become. He lifted the phone and gave a faux groan.

"Hello, mother," Peter said in a strained tone. He smiled at me so that I knew he was toying with her. I could hear bits of Rebecca's voice, but couldn't make out the words.

"I don't know what you thought you were trying to prove," Peter said firmly, "but it went horribly. A yelling match in the middle of the street. I tried to hold her for the authorities." There was a pause as Rebecca's voice chimed in. I could hear the desperation.

"No.. No, she scratched my face to get loose," Peter continued, "I'm sure it will scar." I couldn't take it anymore. I tried to grab the phone and Peter pulled it away. I scooted on top of him, my breasts in his face and used both hands to pin his arm and grab the phone. I was laughing so hard I could hardly speak when Peter finally gave in and let me have it.

"He's torturing you," I laughed into the phone. Peter tickled my side, making me drop the phone on his chest. He grabbed it quickly and put it on speaker.

"You're on speaker, Mom."

"I gather things went well," Rebecca said. I could hear the glee in her voice. I am sure Peter only heard 'I told you so.'

"Very well," we replied in unison. More laughing.

"You don't know how pleased that makes me," Rebecca admitted, "you two belong with each other. I saw that from the beginning. I am sorry I used deceit, but you both seemed intent on screwing it up."

"That reminds me," Peter said, his face becoming serious, "I'm still trying to arrest you. I mean have you arrested."

"You haven't dealt with that?" Rebecca asked.

"We...were talking about...other things," I said. Peter and I shared a smile. I could swear he was blushing.

"Peter, where is your head?" Rebecca scolded. Peter immediately buried his head between my breasts. I tried not to laugh, but it leaked out anyway.

"Mom, we'll take it from here," Peter said, then softened, "and thank you." There was an apology buried in those words.

"You call me if he gives you any trouble, Ella." I could hear the humor in Rebecca's words.

"I will, Mrs. Charming," I answered. I was naked in her son's bed. Using her first name seemed wrong. It was some kind of high school impropriety flashback.

"It's Rebecca, Dear."

"Goodbye, Mother," Peter said. His hands were getting amorous again. Our wrestling for the phone must have set him off. He ended the call before Rebecca could say goodbye. I let him take me, and joyfully he did. As far as I could tell, dancing was his only weakness.

~

"So, tell me everything," Peter asked softly. My head was tucked into his shoulder, one leg over his torso and my hand was making sure his chest didn't have any imperfections. I couldn't remember feeling so good.

"In the beginning God created..." I teased.

"Smart ass," Peter laughed, "everything about how and why you hacked my firewall." I should have been prepared for the question. I was too busy being naked to think of much else. I lifted my head and looked at this eyes. There was nothing but trust in them. Lying would have to be saved for the authorities.

"I can't," I said, "I'm protecting someone." Peter's eyes widened. There was no admonishment, just a strong curiosity.

"Someone else hacked my systems?"

"As a favor to me," I said, then quickly added, "he's never done it before. We didn't think anyone would find out."

"He?" Shit, I let that slip.

"I'm in trouble either way," I paused for a moment, "a family I love very much will be destroyed if this goes past me." Peter's eyes were shifting back and forth between my left and right eye. I waited to see if my trust was well placed. He smiled and kissed me. There was a mountain of trust in that kiss. I hadn't gambled at all.

74

"Tell me what you can," Peter said. I did. Everything about my father's death. Agnus and the will. How I let my pride and envy of my stepsisters drive me to choose an illicit outlet. He listened, his hand played with my hair as I spoke. At times, I wondered if he was really listening or thinking of us instead. He was a computer guy, so I assumed multitasking was ingrained.

"Agnus is a bitch," Peter surmised. He had been listening. "You had no idea that it was my firewall your friend hacked?"

"Nope," I replied, "I was avoiding you at the dance because I thought you might recognize me from the flat tire. I thought it would be embarrassing." Peter laughed. I slapped his chest. Not hard, just enough so he knew my feelings were important.

"I recognized you immediately," Peter admitted, ignoring my slap, "that day in the rain was all I could think of. I was kicking myself for not asking for your number when it happened."

"Why didn't you tell me?"

"I was waiting for you," Peter replied, "I didn't feel right announcing that I already knew how beautiful your breasts were." that earned him a quick kiss, "for a while, I thought you were avoiding me because you remembered and thought me...well...not your cup of tea."

"Not true, my love," I said, stroking the side of his face. Peter was my cup of tea. Green tea. The kind that is not only tasted good but was good for you. He was good for me in so many ways. A few kisses later and I was satisfied he was as sure as I was.

"You get some rest," Peter said, untangling from my arms, "I'll get on the phone and see about undoing what I started." It was actually way past my normal bedtime. His too, I suspected. Visions of falling asleep in his arms were painfully thrust aside. After he leaned down for the last kiss, I watched his naked ass as he left the bedroom. It was a cute butt. I closed my eyes and thought of how the day had progressed. I learned that you can fall asleep smiling.

Not my alarm woke me. It was an annoying chirp that kept repeating at an ever increasing rate. A warm body reached across mine and slammed down on top of the clock. I felt Peter's naked form pull against me under the sheets.

"It's going to go off again in seven minutes," Peter whispered. His lips were so close to my ear it sent a shiver down my neck.

"Mmmm," I moaned as tucked my butt into him. Peter was a wonderful way to wake up. He wrapped his free arm around and pulled me in tight.

"The FBI is looking for you," Peter whispered. My eyes opened. I was awake. "The military thinks the breach was a test for a foreign intrusion into our nation's digital infrastructure."

"Ah..it was a charity dance," I stuttered. I felt physically safe in Peter's arms. Mentally, I was changing my name and running to Bora Bora.

"I know," Peter said, "I guess I was pretty angry when you left and I said things." I turned my head to see his eyes. He looked like a four-year-old who just broke his mother's favorite lamp. "I'm trying to undo it, but the wheels have been turning for a few days."

"What did you say?"

"I thought you deceived me," Peter confessed, "I didn't know you were...you. I was a little irrational."

"Peter, sweetie, what did you say?"

"Something to the effect of; only a foreign government would have the necessary resources to mount such an attack ." Peter shrugged his shoulders guiltily, "I used other words to describe you that I hope you ignore if they get repeated." I was in a world of trouble and all I could do is smile at my four-year-old who was trying to glue the lamp back together.

"Will you visit me in prison?" I joked.

"Ella, this isn't funny," Peter's guilt was hurting him. I rolled my body around, breasts to chest.

"Will you stand by me?" I asked.

"Of course."

"Then I don't care about anything else," I smiled, "I don't care about my inheritance, the FBI or my stepmother." Peter eyes turned loving, "I hear they have conjugal visits in prison," I teased. His lips were just as wonderful as earlier that morning. I looked at the clock and did some quick math. If I got going right then, I could make to work on time. I looked back at Peter.

"I'm going to be late," I decided.

"So am I," Peter said. We made love, interrupted briefly while Peter beat the snot out of the snooze alarm.

~

"*Y*ou're late," Agnus said, her hands on her hips as I got out of the elevator. I smiled at her and ignored her comment. All I could think of was Peter. My body felt light as a feather and the thought of cleaning offices was not depressing. "No excuses?" Agnus stated as I passed by her. I was going to let that comment go, but I was too happy not to share. I turned, my smile growing opposite to her frown.

"I'm in love," I said and then I added something completely inappropriate, "mother." I made it sound like more like 'bitch.' I watched her face turn red. It was incredibly pleasant. Her mouth moved, but nothing came out. I had caught her by surprise. A preemptive sneak attack. I would pay for it later, but right now, I could still smell Peter on me and didn't care about later. I left her there, stunned, and started my night's work.

~

"*Y*ou and Peter Charming?" Raj verified.

"He's wonderful," I said, my euphoria hadn't faded even after cleaning twenty offices. "is this how you feel with Kiran?" I smiled.

"That the rest of the world could fall into a bottomless pit and it doesn't matter?" Raj returned.

"Yes, that's it."

"Kiran makes me feel that way," Raj said, "Aanya brings us right back to caring that the world doesn't fall away." The thought of a family drifted into my mind. It was too soon to think of such things though the idea of sharing Peter with a son or daughter was not unpleasant.

"The FBI is looking for me and I don't even care," I said, letting my joy fill the room.

"The FBI!" Raj said as he turned quickly from his workstation, "That is the worst thing that could happen. I never wanted it go this far." His face was losing all its color.

"It doesn't matter, Raj. Peter will stand by me and that's all that matters." I had a humorous vision of Peter standing before me, swinging a sword to protect my honor. I had no idea where all the thoughts were coming from, but they were wonderful.

"FBI means prison," Raj continued, "I can't let you do that."

"You can and you will," I said firmly, "This whole mess was my choice and I got Peter out of it. There's no way you are going ruin it by getting your family deported."

"I don't feel good about this," Raj rambled on, "it is not right and honor says I step in."

"Your honor is for Kiran and Aanya," I said, "I will be fine. If anything does come of this, it is my first offense. I doubt it will amount to much." And Peter will stand by me. The FBI is looking for me and I could do nothing but smile. My phone vibrated. It was a text from Peter.

I would really love to skip breakfast again

me too

6?

pick me up?

hard to work - too happy - see you at 6

kisses

I just scheduled sex. I had never done that before. I had accepted dates that I figured would become sexual, but never a flat out naked appointment. I laughed at my phone. If it was anyone but Peter, I would have thought it slutish. With him, it was so damned perfect and felt absolutely appropriate. It was all too much fun. The rest of the world could fall into a bottomless pit for all I cared.

"Is that Peter?" Raj asked. He still seemed depressed about the FBI.

"Yes," I said, then added a white lie, "he wants to pick me up for breakfast this morning."

"Does he know about me?"

"Not you personally, but yes, he knows I don't have the knowledge to hack the firewalls," I replied.

"He must think me a coward," Raj said, his eyes finding the floor.

"No," I said softly, "he thinks I value your friendship enough to not destroy your family."

"I will not forgive myself if you end up in prison," Raj mumbled.

"You must," I said, "for Kiran and Aanya. If it was just you, I would have told the FBI long ago." Raj looked up and saw my smile. At least my joke lightened the mood. I changed the subject to trivial things. I knew Raj hadn't forgotten about the FBI, but at least he was willing to let it go for now.

I spent some time in the bathroom trying to clean up before Peter arrived. I felt rather pleased with myself and the way life was going. I thought my life wouldn't really begin until I was thirty-two with my freedom from Agnus. Now, that was merely another birthday. My life began the previous morning, when Peter was too close to hate me.

I undid my pony tail and ran a feeble comb through my hair. It took a while to break through the tangles, creating organized lines that looked softer. I suppressed a laugh knowing it would soon be a mess again. I touched up my mascara and brushed the lint off my clothes. I liked the smiling woman in the mirror. It had been a long time since she was my friend.

Agnus was waiting for me when I exited the bathroom, wearing a superior smile. That I could ignore. The men in suits next to her, I could not.

"You have surprised me," Agnus said, then she added, "daughter." It was laced with as much bitch as she could muster. "These gentlemen seem to think you have an alias. Now, I said, not my little Ella. Tell me it's not so." Her smile grew as she stepped off to the side. Out of everything that happened, her glee was the most irritating thing.

"Ella Tremaine, you're under arrest for wire fraud and espionage," the taller suit said. My eyes widened. "Please turn around and place your hands behind your back."

"I need to make a call," I said. An unexpected begging invaded my voice. I felt fear. Espionage. That was quite a bit more serious than I had expected.

"Sorry, ma'am," the shorter suit said, "the warrant is explicit. No communications or contact with any technology."

"I have rights," I demanded.

"National security trumps those rights," tall suit said. He moved toward me. I thought he intended to forcibly cuff me if I didn't comply. I turned and put my hands behind my back. I couldn't help it, my hands were shaking.

"I haven't seen a badge," I stammered. What rights did I have? Tall suit turned me around once my hands were secure.

"Agent Dawson, FBI," tall suit said as he held his badge so I could read it. I guess I had some rights.

"Agent Phillips, NSA," the shorter man said, holding up a different badge. My knees went weak. I was in more trouble than I knew.

"It was only a dance," I whimpered.

"This way, Ms. Tremaine," Dawson said. Agnus was covering her mouth. She was hiding a smile. I no longer cared about her little victory. I was concerned for my freedom.

"Agnus, I need a lawyer," I stated as Dawson took my arm and led me to the elevator. She was my purse. My finances were drained by a flat tire and shoes I only wore once.

"I'll see what I can do," Agnus said with a chuckle in her throat. I was sure she was going to hire someone straight out of school. The elevator opened and the agents and I stepped in. When I turned around, Raj was standing down the hall, his face ashen. I straightened up and tried to look strong. I subtly shook my head. Thankfully, he didn't move. At least his family would be unscathed.

Agent Dawson read me my rights on the way down. It was more frightening than I could have imagined. There was no innocent-until-proven-guilty in his tone. They placed me in the back of a blue sedan and, once I was buckled, pulled out into traffic.

"Where are you taking me?"

"FBI offices, Ms. Tremaine," Phillips said, turning in the passenger seat to look at me, "it would be in your best interest to cooperate, though you can choose to remain silent." He shook his head, "I would think that unwise for a person in your position."

"I went to a dance," I repeated, "it was stupid, but I'm not a spy or anything."

"We can recognize a trial run," Phillips continued, "you purposely compromised a military grade firewall and tried to ingratiate yourself with its creator." He shook his head again. "It is my understanding that you laid the seeds for you conquest by flaunting yourself prior to the dance. A seemingly random encounter that defies coincidence."

"It was a flat tire," I begged, "I didn't plan anything."

"What was it that turned you?" Phillips continued, "tired of waiting for your inheritance." My eyes widened at his knowledge, "Yes, we have an extensive file on you. Impatient spoiled rich girl. As we speak, your home and car are being searched. It would better for you if you came clean and told us who you work for."

"No one," I insisted quickly, "I was envious of my stepsisters. I'll admit that, but I would never do anything against America."

Phillips turned to Dawson and shared a smile. "They are all suddenly patriots when it's time to pay the piper." Dawson chuckled. I was in over my head.

"I want a lawyer," I begged, "you said I could have a lawyer present." At least that's what Dawson said when he read me my rights.

"Then they go all stubborn," Phillips chuckled. He turned back to me. "I dislike people like you. You trample all over your country then demand the same rights you work so hard to destroy." There was an unwavering hate in his eyes. My eyes began to well up. Handcuffed, I couldn't even wipe the shame away. Phillips rolled his eyes, "and then they try the crying thing."

Unbidden, my eyes began to drain down my cheeks. I needed Peter.

~

*W*aiting was the hardest part. I sat on a hard metal chair, handcuffed to a metal table that was bolted to the floor. The room was empty except for an empty chair on the other side of the table and two cameras mounted on the ceiling in opposite corners. Not even a clock to know how long I had been there. I only knew it had been hours.

I was strip searched when I arrived by two rough female agents who thought less of me than Phillips did. With rubber gloves, they probed to find secrets I didn't carry. The humiliation brought more tears. I tried desperately to remain strong, but each time I found my backbone, they crushed it again. I was hungry, thirsty and I really needed to pee. Instead, I sat on the rock hard chair and tried not to break down.

"Good afternoon, Ms. Tremaine," A woman said as she entered the room, "I am Agent Stratford with the FBI." She smiled and placed a thick folder on the table. Her dark brown hair was cropped short and she had an athletic build. Unlike the suits earlier, she was more casual in her brown slacks and tan blouse. Her badge was hanging off her belt.

"I have to use the bathroom," I said desperately. Surely, a woman would understand.

"We'll get to your needs after you answer a few questions," Stratford stated as she sat in the empty chair and opened the folder. On top of the papers was my pink phone in a plastic bag. The more I thought about it, the more I needed to pee.

"I am confused," Stratford continued as if my bladder wasn't her concern, "you have little money," I watched her removing papers from the folder, my bank statements among them, "yet you were able to finance a $5,000 a plate ball." She chuckled a little, "I thought my finances were bad until I got a look at yours." They hadn't traced the money back to Tremaine Marketing, Inc. Raj had hidden his tracks well. I could never tell them where the money came from.

"I really have to pee," I said.

"I really need an answer," Stratford said, leaning back in her chair. Her smile told me that she meant to hold me there until I complied. I remained silent and pushed my legs together to try and quell the urge.

"Whatever government you're working for will deny you even exist," Stratford continued, "your loyalty to them is now unfounded. We are the only ones who can help you now."

"Don't I get a lawyer?" I asked. Maybe a lawyer could get me the bathroom.

"In time," Stratford said, "but do you really want to give up your chance at leniency? Speak to us now and it will be taken into consideration at sentencing." They already had me convicted in their minds. "Who financed this operation? Who compromised the firewall?" she looked back down at the folder full of paper and waved her hand over it, "there is nothing here that even indicates you know how to turn a computer on. We know you are working for another organization." I crossed my legs and squeezed them tight.

"It was a dance," I pleaded, "I hacked the firewall myself. I just wanted to go to the dance." My bladder felt like it was going to burst. "Please let me go to the bathroom."

"Give me the password to the phone," Stratford said, holding the phone up. "They tell me the encryption is something new. Are you trying to tell me you created it as well?"

"I...I forgot the password," I stammered. I hated lying, but Raj's texts and voicemail were on the thing.

"Where did you get the money?" Stratford yelled, slamming the phone down. "Do you think we're stupid?" My eyes betrayed me again. I didn't want to break down in front of her, but I couldn't think quick enough to stall the fear. "Do you know what prison will be like? Traitors are dealt with harshly." I dropped my head down to my cuffed hands to wipe away the tears.

"I have to go to the bathroom," I cried.

"Who are you working for?" Stratford yelled louder, "You tell me what I need to know or you will rot as a slave to 300-pound dyke in prison." The floodgates opened and I lost control of my bladder. Stratford scooted back quickly as the puddle grew beneath the table. I no longer knew if I was crying for my freedom or the fact that she made me pee myself. I never felt so weak in my life.

The door opened and a man poked his head in. "Shit," the man said, "get her cleaned up fast." I lifted my head. "Get those damn cuffs off her."

"Give me ten more minutes," Stratford said, her smile was bordering on evil. I prayed he wouldn't give her ten more seconds.

"I doubt you have thirty seconds," the man warned, "her lawyers are here." Plural? Agnus sent more than one. A ray of hope.

"Keep them out!" Stratford argued.

"You do it," the man complained, "they're from the top firms in the city. I got the division head wanting to know why they haven't seen their client. I can't fight politics." Stratford looked at me with anger. I think she saw herself saving the free world. I was strengthened by the thought of lawyers and firms. I couldn't believe that Agnus pulled out all the stops. Maybe I misjudged her.

"It was just a dance," I said stronger. I liked that some sense of control had returned. "I'm going to need some clean clothes, or is that against the rules." I wiped the rest of my tears away. The fear in man's face gave me courage. I had lawyers.

"Uncuff her," a man in a very expensive black suit with a blue tie demanded. He looked at the floor and I saw his temples pulse. "Is this your idea of proper procedure?" he said, looking at the two agents. He had a touch of gray on his sideburns with perfectly groomed short black hair.

"Brendan Mcelroy of Finnegan, Roy, and Clausland," the man introduced himself to me, "I have been retained as part of your counsel team, Ms. Tremaine. That is, of course, if you agree." Stratford was moving with acuity, ignoring the mess on the floor in an attempt to get the cuffs off. I smiled as relief washed over me.

"Yes, please," I replied. I could have kissed him if I wasn't sitting in a pool of urine. Stratford released me from the cuffs and I resisted the urge to stand. Brendan recognized my hesitancy and took a step back.

"Please secure an unmonitored room so we may confer with our client," Brendan ordered. He had an authority about him that made you want to comply. "I expect her there shortly after she has had a chance to freshen up. I also expect a copy of the video of the inter- rogation," he added pointing to the cameras. Stratford's face lost its color. I felt better.

Stratford hustled to get me into the bathroom. There was no apology or contrition, but a definite shift in power had occurred. I was innocent until proven guilty again. It was the agent's bathroom, complete with lockers and showers. Stratford supplied me with a towel and some soap. After grunting out some instructions about not touching the lockers, she left to get me some dry clothes.

The shower was heavenly warm. I was human again. It took a few minutes before I was sure the last traces of the accident were gone. I succeeded in keeping my hair mostly dry which was surprising since I had an urge to douse myself and let the warm water shield me from the world.

Stratford returned with brand new, still in the package, FBI sweats. I would have to go commando, but clean and dry was better than wet and smelly. I dressed quickly and asked politely to be brought to my lawyers. Stratford complied without verbal acknowledgment. I could tell that the situation was killing her on the inside.

"I am sorry we did not get here sooner," Brendan said. I looked at the four faces of obviously successful lawyers. Three men and one woman dressed as if they had just stepped out of a catalog.

"I am so happy you came when you did," I said, "I'm just surprised my stepmother responded at all." There were a few confused looks.

"We have been retained by the Charmings," Brendan responded, "is there a problem with that." I think my smiled convinced them there wasn't. Screw Agnus. Peter loves me.

"Let's see about getting you out of here," Brendan said. Introductions were made and my interrogation discussed. I informed them that I did request to go to the bathroom multiple times and did request a lawyer. Dollar signs ignited in their eyes, but all I wanted was to get out of there. I didn't want to sue the FBI or anyone else for that matter. I especially didn't want a courtroom full of people see me pee myself.

There was a knock at the door. A female agent I didn't recognize entered with a folder and an uncomfortable expression. "The recording equipment didn't seem to be working during the interview," she said. I rolled my eyes. My attorneys saw red.

"You disallowed my client an attorney, chained her to a table and didn't allow her to use the bathroom for what...three, four hours?" Brendan seethed, "and now you tell us you have no record of it."

"I am not aware of any illegal or inhumane treatment, sir," the agent claimed, "I am only stating that the recording equipment was not working."

"I wonder if agent Stratford would like to be subpoenaed," Brendan added.

"National security allows us great leeway," the agent said.

"Not that great, and certainly not with American citizens on American soil," Brendan informed her, "If you wish Ms. Tremaine to not pursue the issues involved with the interview, I suggest you move quickly on a bond hearing. I am sure there are judges that will recognize Ms. Tremaine has no priors and isn't a flight risk." My lawyers all glared at the agent. There was no fear in their eyes, but I saw plenty in the agent. I folded my hands across my chest and added my confident stare as well.

It was four hours later before I found myself exiting FBI headquarters. About twenty years earlier than Agent Stratford would have preferred. The judge found the espionage linkage weak but agreed that the wire fraud charge was relevant. A $10,000 bail was paid by Brendan on behalf of the Charmings. I had to agree to stay off all computers and not leave the city without informing the FBI.

I would have hated the building itself if it wasn't for what I saw slumped in an uncomfortable chair in the foyer as I was leaving. A tired, frustrated and oh so beautiful Peter. HIs eyes brightened and a smile emerged as he saw me approaching. His arms and lips were just as I remembered.

"Why are you in FBI sweats?" Peter asked.

"Can we get out here first?"

"Yes...Yes, we can," Peter said enthusiastically. My hand in his, he led me out of my mini nightmare.

~

"So, they think you're a spy?" Peter asked. He was scrambling eggs while I was laying bacon across a pan. I hadn't realized how hungry I was until he mentioned food. I liked that idea of cooking with him. It was wonderfully domestic and a little charming that he thought of my needs.

"You can't imagine how happy I was to see the lawyers," I said, leaning over to kiss his cheek. I liked making him smile. "a few more minutes in that room with that woman, and I would have claimed to have shot Kennedy." I didn't think we could be any closer. Our shoulders kept rubbing against each other was we worked. We weren't even taking the trouble to make it look unintentional.

"Raj wants to confess," Peter said. I sucked in my breath.

"How do you know about Raj?"

"He found me on the street looking for you," Peter admitted, "I guess he knew we were supposed to meet this morning. He told me what happened and pretty much told me everything else."

"Oh, Peter," I begged, "you can't let him confess. They will deport his family and things won't go well for them in India. They are the best friends I have and I don't want to lose them."

"Deport him?" Peter smiled, "I want to hire him. He's brilliant and thinks way out of the box. The way he tricked my firewall into thinking the packet streams were authorized was ingenious. He sees holes where the rest of us see solid walls."

"You like him too," I summarized.

"Yes," Peter said, his eyes looking up as he thought, "I think I do."

"Good," I agreed, "his wife and daughter don't need to be brought into this. I am in trouble either way."

"I think my ranting made this worse," Peter said as he moved to the stove and poured the eggs into a pan.

"I should have never run out of the dance," I confessed. Peter saw me coming with the bacon and opened the oven door. No need for words, we were in cooking sync. I placed the bacon the middle rack and Peter closed the door.

"Yay, I took that badly," Peter admitted.

"But you rescued me today," I said. I put my hand over his and we stirred the eggs together with a wooden spoon. Highly inefficient, but so nice.

"I wish I could have found you sooner. I would have liked to spare you the interrogation," Peter said as his lips moved closer to mine. I ran my hand up his arm and behind his neck and pulled him closer. I wanted to let the eggs burn and let the intimacy continue. Every moment of our joined lips increased his passion. I heard the spoon fall free as he wrapped me in his arms.

"We are going to starve to death at this rate," Peter whispered into my mouth. I could feel his lips curving against mine. Starvation wouldn't be so bad, but the loss of stamina might slow us down. I pulled myself away. Not far away - still touching. I didn't want to lose the closeness.

"Food first," I said, struggling to lessen my smile. I told my body to put the tingle that was growing on hold. I saw a shiver run down Peter's spine. He was feeling what I was. There was more in sync than cooking.

"Are you going to work tonight," Peter asked.

"Without sleep," I said, shaking me head no, "I have some time off I can use." Peter's smile grew and he stirred the eggs more vigorously.

"I was thinking of taking the night off as well," Peter said. His eyes weren't looking at me, almost if he were afraid of his salacious thoughts.

"Are you planning to take advantage of an exhausted woman?" I teased.

"Well, now that your resistance is down, I thought I would lull you into a false sense of security with a backrub."

"Mmmm."

"Then...once your muscles become lazy and useless, I figured I would lead the first dance," Peter smiled as he stirred. The eggs were beginning to clump. "A slow dance to start. Something that requires very little movement on your part. I was planning on having my way with you." He smiled, "I have never seduced an international spy before."

"You intend to learn all my secrets?" The tingle wasn't listening to my brain anymore. I knew I should eat something, but the thought of food was becoming less important.

"Everyone of them," Peter teased, "hopefully, even ones you don't know about." The idea of naked exploration blossomed in my mind. It should have scared me. With Peter, it sounded so wonderful. My trust was his for the taking.

"Those eggs done yet?" I asked too quickly.

"Almost," Peter replied, "what about the bacon?" I had forgotten all about it. We scooted our feet back and I pulled the oven door down and peeked inside. The four pieces were sizzling well as the smell of bacon filled the room. They were still on the rubbery side of done.

"Oven mitts?" I asked. Peter pointed to a drawer where I found two fat red mittens. I pulled the pan out and flipped the bacon. I replaced the pan in the oven while Peter was moving the eggs to plates.

"Bacon has a few more minutes," I complained.

"Ahh, the smell of bacon and a beautiful woman," Peter quipped, "I do believe I have found heaven." I had to laugh. I tried not to, but he seemed so proud of his silly humor. How could a beautiful woman not laugh?

~

*P*eter was true to his word. The massage was wonderfully slow and turned my muscles into wet noodles. He leaned down every once in awhile to tease my ears with his lips, whispering tender things to make sure I was awake. His fingers were firm, yet gentle as they glided around my back. Sometimes he would find a knot and spent extra care to rub it out always followed by a loving kiss. I could barely form words and mostly moaned my encouragement.

I rolled over and tried to rise to thank him properly when it was over. He pushed my lazy body back to the bed. It wasn't over. He lightly kissed my lips then trailed off to the side of my neck. Soft wet kisses trailed down my neck, climbed my breasts and concentrated on my nipples. His tongue tickled, mixing a chuckle into my moans. His kisses continued down my tummy. I closed my eyes as he slowly made his way between my legs.

There are certain pleasures in life that defy description. The senses mash the feelings, sights and sounds together into a ball of lovely luxury that defies recall. Peter found all my secrets. Had I been a spy, I would have betrayed all. His sweet tongue teased little strings of bliss tied to my core. My hips rose off the bed when the pleasure could no longer be contained. My entire body stiffened as pure joy invaded every crevice of my being.

I was half laughing, half crying when reality slowly crawled back.

Little bursts of pleasure exploded, fighting the return of normalcy. Then, as if a switch was thrown, pleasure became a ticklish torture. Laughing I tried to squirm away from Peter's tongue. I could hear his soft laugh as he continued the torment.

"Stop," I cried, laughing so hard the word barely came out. Peter did. His face rose with a grin that was both proud and happy. I reached down and pulled him up my quivering body. "Such a lovely man," I complimented. If this was life with Peter, I wanted more.

I reached between us when we kissed. His excitement was strong. I spread my legs and guided him into me. I exhaled as my parts found their perfect match. Peter's smile faded to a dreamy expression that said more than any words ever could.

"I'm yours," Peter whispered.

"And I'm yours," I repeated as my eyes watered. He moved slowly like he intended it to last forever. I desired it to last a lifetime. We cemented the 'us' in that coupling. Sex was no longer just sex.

∽

"Can you call my mother?" Peter asked. We were laying in bed enjoying each other in the peaceful afterglow of our sharing. I reached over and wiped away a drop of sweat that threatened Peter's eye. We must have burnt off a ton of calories.

"Your mother?" I returned. I wondered if my hair looked as wild as his right now. It was incredible cute the way it exploded off his head in wrong directions. It was even better knowing I was the cause of its calamity.

"I promised I would call as soon as you were released," Peter admitted, "she'll rip me a new one if I call her now." I smiled.

"You would prefer she yell at me?"

"In truth, yes," Peter smiled back. He reached forward and tucked an errant strand of my hair behind my ear. "but she won't yell at you."

"Are you afraid of your own mother?"

"Terrified," Peter laughed, "it's that grating tone of disappointment she can put into her words. She mixes it with a blend of I-told-you-so. It can be very emasculating."

"She loves you dearly," I said.

"And that's what makes it so effective." Peter pulled me closer. He cared little that I was as sweaty as he.

"For you, I will make the call," I feigned capitulation. That earned me some loving kisses. I would have gotten them anyways, but it is always sweeter when you earn them.

Peter disappeared into the bathroom when I rang Rebecca. Her tone changed immediately when she realized I was on Peter's phone. She listened intently as I retold my arrest saga. I left out the peeing part figuring she didn't need to know a weakling was dating her son.

"So it was a horrible day," Rebecca summarized. I had already forgotten the emotions prior to seeing Peter in the lobby of the FBI building. I smiled thinking of Peter saving me and discovering all my secrets. He was mine.

"Actually," I said slowly, trying to find the right words for a mother, "it was...Peter turned it into one the best days of my life." There. Might as well own up to the truth. There was silence on the other line. I said too much. "Rebecca..." There was a tone that indicated another call on the line. It wasn't my phone, but I found the ignore button quickly enough. 'Gen Rickers,' whoever that was, would just have to wait.

"Do you love him?" Rebecca asked. It was asked quietly, almost as if she were afraid to ask. I was now afraid to answer.

"Yes," I answered with the same lack of enthusiasm.

"That is the most wonderful thing I've heard in a long time," Rebecca stuttered. She was crying. So many tears today and somehow my eyes found more.

"He is kind of wonderful," I slobbered out.

"I've been waiting for someone to figure that out," Rebecca slurred. The conversation deteriorated into words half spoken, but totally understood. If anyone would have been listening, they would have thought us mentally challenged. We ended the call with a promise to talk later, over lunch perhaps.

I wiped my eyes for the umpteenth time and promptly pushed the wrong button on Peter's phone. Instead of turning it dark, I initiated the voicemail from the call I ignored. The VCR controls were in a different position from my phone and they took me a moment to locate. My heart fell and I never pushed stop as the words began to resonate.

Charming, this is Rickers. FBI surveillance has informed me that you have taken an interest in Ella Tremaine. That is a breach of our security agreement and we are within our rights to void your contract with armed services. Cease all contact with Ms.Tremaine and contact my office immediately. We may yet preserve the contract and prevent a lot of headaches on both sides.

The voice was authoritative. 'Gen' was most likely 'General.' I had ruined myself, risked Raj's family and now I was destroying Peter. I was a curse. I put the phone down with shaking hands. Quietly, I started to dress.

"Going somewhere?" Peter asked. I turned to tell him I had to leave. His eyes wouldn't let me. He was too close. I stopped putting my shoes on. All I could offer was weak tears. Peter rushed over and folded me in his arms. I pointed at the phone.

"What did my mother say?" Peter demanded. I shook my head.

"It's the voicemail," I said weakly. I watched his face go ashen as he listened. He slammed the phone down when the message was done. He stood and walked across the room and stood near the door. I could hear him taking deep breaths. When he turned, his face was red and I saw anger in his eyes.

"Those assholes are following you," He said in a deep voice, "I'll not have you spied on." His hand slammed on the dresser for emphasis. Spied upon. Did he not hear the same message I did?

"I'm wrecking your business," I said, "I can't do that to you."

"Fuck the business," Peter shouted. This was irrational Peter. The shock of his outburst scared me and I jerked away involuntarily. Peter's eyes changed and he visibly calmed at my reaction. He slowly moved forward and knelt before the bed I was sitting on. "Fuck the business," he repeated quietly, "I don't want it if it means losing you."

"I can't ruin you," I said. He took my hand in his.

"Ruin me?" Peter smiled, "the only way you could do that is to leave me." He kissed the back of my hand softly. "I'm not in this for a minute, an hour, or a day. I want you forever. To hell with the rest of the world."

"The rest of the world could fall into a bottomless pit and it doesn't matter," I whispered back. How I loved his lips. Forgiveness, love and passion seeped from his lips to mine. A hurricane could have swept through and I wouldn't have known.

"What did my mother say?" Peter asked. With all the problems we were facing, it was my conversation with his mother he was worried about.

"She wants to have lunch with me soon," I said, unable to describe the conversation.

"See, she won't yell at you," Peter said with happiness. I think I was just promoted to mother-buffer.

"What are we going to do?" I asked, not wanting to break the spell, but desperately hoping he had a plan.

"Well... we aren't going to hide," Peter said, "we'll face up to what was done and hopefully the truth will override the speculation."

"But your business."

"You are my business," Peter said, picking up his phone. He hit a few buttons and put it to his ear. He had a sly smile on his face.

"You're not doing something stupid?" I asked. He nodded yes, but the way his hand stroked the side of my face I could only smile.

"Evening General." There was a pause while Peter listened.

"Well that's going to be a problem." another pause.

"It looks like you'll need to go out for another procurement." Peter's smile grew and he winked at me.

"Sorry General, I love the lady." Now I was smiling. Peter's eyebrows gave a little bounce. "by the way, I have a line on how the firewall was breached. I'll probably have the only product that can thwart that type of attack. But, rules are rules. Have fun with the new procurement." Peter was almost giddy when he disconnected.

"Raj told you how," I said.

"Not all of it," Peter admitted, "but Rickers doesn't know that." I had to laugh. No sleep, rollercoaster emotions all day, made the laughter a bit more than it should have been. Peter took in stride and joined. Truly, it was us against the world.

# THE WEEKS THAT FOLLOWED WERE
## WONDERFULLY STRANGE

The weeks that followed were wonderfully strange. Agnus had put me on indefinite suspension from work. An unpaid vacation of sorts. There were clauses in the employee handbook that applied to personnel that did not present a good moral character. She made sure I understood that my job depended upon the results of the criminal case against me. I would have flat out *q*uit, but the suspension seemed to cause Agnus more work. It was petty but pleasing. I no longer desired to wait seven more years.

The FBI had a constant tail on me. They were so sure I was working for a foreign government, I couldn't even get my mail without a photo being taken. Peter and I learned to recognize them. They always traveled in twos. I suspected that was necessary so they could keep each other awake. My life wasn't exactly 007 *q*uality. Being put on my detail was probably a punishment.

Peter and I started to go out more. We figured a life in bed would warp us in the long run. We found interesting places to eat. The more obscure the better, just to tease our followers. Peter had fun sending out plates of au dourness to our shadows. In time, we waved and they waved back. We invented names for them as we began to recognize them by face. I wondered how many real criminals were running loose because of the wasted resources.

Rebecca invited me to a luncheon. I thought she intended a one on one but was surprised when I saw two other women sitting at the table. Rebecca had chosen a fancy tea room, The Green Leaf. It was obviously designed to please female senses. There were ten women to every male and most of those males looked uncomfortable.

As I approached the table, I was met by two smiles I recognized. Ruth and Betty were sipping tea. Ruth treating the cup as if it was fragile and Betty like she was drinking from a mug.

"Hello Cindy," Betty said loudly. The teasing in her tone was not lost on me. Ruth scowled at her and smiled at me as she patted the seat next to her.

"Hello, Ruth, Betty," I said as I sat down between Ruth and Rebecca, "thank you for inviting me, Rebecca." I was little nervous knowing I owed these two an apology. "I'm sorry about the dance," I started.

"I'm not," Betty interrupted,"it was the most exciting party we went to all year." Ruth actually laughed. I think it was more for my benefit than Betty's.

"I've brought them both up to date," Rebecca said. "I thought it might be nice to have some friends in case you end up at another of those functions." She said 'in case' but she meant 'when.' It would be one of the requirements for being with Peter. Not a bad one either.

"So, are they following you now, Ella?" Betty asked leaning forward and dropping her voice so the other tables couldn't hear. Her interest was real. She liked the cloak and dagger stuff. Ruth didn't admonish her, so I suspected she was interested as well.

"Tom and Jerry are parked right outside," I said, "at least that's what Peter and I have named them. One is short and the other is a bean pole."

"I've never met an FBI agent," Betty continued.

"And were not starting now," Ruth injected. Betty liked to stir the pot.

"What kind of car are they driving?" Betty asked. Ruth rolled her eyes. Rebecca covered her smile with her hand.

"Black SUV. A Cherokee I think, " I answered. Betty rose and walked over to one of the front windows, ignoring the full table of customers she had to maneuver around. "What is she planning?" I asked Ruth.

"Heaven only knows," Ruth said, "she never grew up." Her lips curled, "one of the reasons I love her so." We watched as Betty spotted the car and then promptly left the tea room.

"My, she is in a mood," Rebecca commented.

"So...you and Peter," Ruth said, ignoring her partner's departure, "Rebecca was telling me that you two fancy each other." Ruth had a way of turning back the clock 100 years. Rebecca became extra attentive.

"He is my one," I replied to Ruth, "I am his," I directed to Rebecca. All kinds of happiness appeared on Rebecca's face. She reached for my hand and grasped it. Visions of what it would have been like growing up with my true mother appeared in my mind. The part of my life that was always missing became more pronounced, and yet less empty.

"I told you it was real," Rebecca said to Ruth, "I saw it in Peter's eyes at the cotillion. Have you ever seen him on the dance floor before?" She turned back to me, "you have his heart. That means you have mine as well."

"I don't know what to say," I admitted. My smile forcing it's way to the surface.

"Peter has needed someone for a long time," Ruth said, "Somehow, he lost track of what was important and put everything into his business. Too nice of a boy to marry a corporation."

"I'm afraid our relationship is damaging his business, " I added, "the military thinks I am a security risk." Rebecca patted my hand.

"Happiness first, work second," Rebecca said, then a sly smile formed, "and how do you feel about children." I felt my face flush. I hadn't gotten that far in my thought process. I always envisioned one or two. Two if at least one was like Aanya.

"We haven't gotten that far," I said, knowing that was a future conversation I needed to have with Peter.

"I'm not holding you to a decision," Rebecca said, "Just asking if you see yourself as a mother." I nodded yes, my face on fire. "Grandchildren!" Rebecca said a little too loud. She acted as if I was pregnant.

"I haven't talked with Peter about that," I whispered, "we haven't talked about the future past my trial."

"It's not leaving this table, dear," Rebecca assured me, "I'm just trying to imagine Peter as a father. It would change him...for the better."

"He would be a good one, " I smiled.

"The best," Ruth agreed and then her expression changed, "She didn't." We followed her eyes to the front door. Betty was leading Tom and Jerry toward our table. Rebecca chuckled at Ruth's surprised expression.

"May I present agents William Henderson and Frank Dolchee," Betty introduced first the short, then the tall agent.

"Ms. Tremaine," William said with a nod followed by Franks nod. Betty introduced Ruth and Rebecca and then asked the waiter to bring two more chairs and place sets to the table.

"I assured them that we would talk scandalously so they could take notes, " Betty said.

"I'm sorry you got stuck following me around," I said.

"It's our job, Ms. Tremaine," Frank said in an apologetic tone, "as we told Betty, we've become convinced it's a waste of time." Betty looked so proud of herself. Ruth was trying to decide to smile or scowl. Rebecca was truly amused.

"Ella, please," I said, "I hope I haven't made it too difficult."

"No Ma'am," William said, then his voice dropped to a whisper, "and that Calamari you and Mr. Charming sent out last night was delicious. Never thought I would like squid." I laughed. At least the entire FBI wasn't out to get me.

"Isn't this against the rules?" Rebecca asked.

"We're paying for our own lunch," Frank said, "so it is more of a violation of the flavor of the rules. Technically, we're still conducting surveillance." Ruth gave up and chuckled.

Betty spent lunch coaxing out FBI stories from Frank and William. It turns out the job is mostly boring with small bits of excitement mixed in. William had only pulled his gun out of its holster once. Frank once tasered a suspect but never unholstered his weapon. Most of their work was white collar crime, limited to people who would surrender to a badge. They had first thought I would be an exciting case, but that wore off *q*uickly. My life wasn't as exciting as they had hoped.

After that lunch, I stopped driving through yellow lights. I was afraid my shadows would lose me or cause an accident trying to make the light. I had no desire to make their life more difficult than it was. Peter, on the other hand, thought the yellow lights were fun.

My court date was approaching *q*uickly. The government had it on the fast track and I instructed my lawyers, against their advice, to not delay. I saw no need in delaying. I wanted it all to end as *q*uickly as possible. I had a new life to build.

Peter was off at meetings, I assumed trying to repair the business I had damaged. I promised him a home cooked meal and I had decided to go gourmet. I was exiting an upscale fishery with a couple of fresh sablefish steaks. I heard my name called just as I approached my car. I turned and found Rayburn violating my comfort zone. It was then that I realized he had called me Cindy.

"Long time, girl," Rayburn said in his over confident tone.

"Hello, Raymond," I said. Mistake. Never acknowledge an idiot.

"I knew you would remember me," Rayburn said, his hand closing around my elbow with way too much familiarity.

"I wish I had time to talk," I lied, "I have to get this fish into the fridge before it spoils. It's good to see you again though." I maneuvered my elbow out of his grasp. I tried to open the car door, but he was too close. "Excuse me," I smiled.

"Maybe you should let the fish spoil," Rayburn said, his smile growing, "let me take you out to eat. We'll hit a club. If I remember, you owe me a dance." He moved closer. The strong scent of alcohol was on his breath.

"Please Rayburn," I said, trying to keep it light, "I need to get home. I promised Peter dinner." I figured that the mention of Peter would end the discussion. I was wrong.

"That stick in the mud," Rayburn continued, "he doesn't know how to treat women." He moved closer, pushing me against my car. I held the wrapped fish between us. A horribly flimsy shield. "I'll make you queen for the night. Rock your world."

"No!" I said loudly. I pushed him back. He was stronger than he looked and barely moved in inch. He laughed as if it were a game. His eyes were tinged in a drunken red.

"No always means yes," Rayburn chuckled.

"No means no," A deep voice said. Franks large hand closed on Rayburn's shoulder and pulled him away. William immediately put himself between Rayburn and me.

"Who the fuck are you two," Rayburn demanded. It looked like he was considering a fight.

"Agents Henderson and Dolchee," William said with authority, flashing his badge and exposing his side arm, "FBI." I smiled at my heroes.

"May I suggest a cab, Sir," Frank said, pulling Rayburn farther away from me. I heard Rayburn mumble something back as he allowed Frank to escort him down the street. I let out the breath I was holding.

"Thank you," I said to William.

"Finally, some excitement," William laughed. Frank joined a moment later with a proud smile.

"Mr. Funderland has decided to call it a day and head home," Frank said, "I hope he didn't ruin yours."

"He tried," I said, "but not with America's finest on duty. I don't know how I can thank you."

"It was kind of nice stopping a crime before it was committed," Frank said, "maybe you could stir up some more trouble to give us something else to do."

"I'll see what I can do," I laughed. Frank and William smiled, said goodbye and headed to their car. I watched them go, thankful that they were there. I wasn't sure how I would have handled a drunk

Rayburn if they weren't. I smiled to myself. Frank and William slid from the acquaintance to the friend category. I held back a chuckle as I realized I liked them following me.

"That bastard," Peter said when I told him about Rayburn.

"He was drunk," I calmed him, "I don't think it would have gone too far. Besides, I think Frank and William scared him pretty good."

"Tom and Jerry still downstairs?" Peter asked.

"They're on until 7:00, I think." Peter smiled and grabbed his phone. I laughed as he ordered the two a large pizza and drinks. I had no idea how many rules we were breaking, but friends took care of friends. Damn the rules.

~

*M*y trial was a week away. I had almost fully moved in with Peter and his parents now considered me family. His father, Daniel, was a workaholic, but took plenty of time out to make sure I was welcome. He, like his wife, had little concern how I had met Peter. Peter was happy and that's all that seemed to matter. Which was good, since that is all that mattered to me.

I went home to gather more of my clothes. I have been moving them piecemeal into Peter's condo. He had given me an entire closet and half the dresser drawers. There was no ring, no ceremony, no license, but we were married in the heart. We started and ended each day with a kiss and shared the bathroom like we had been together our whole lives. More importantly, we could make each other laugh. We didn't even need words anymore. Something would strike my eyes as funny and a quick look at Peter would set him off as well. A wonderful connection I never wanted to see go away.

Agnus, unfortunately, was home. Her smile told me she would attempt to ruin my day. I tried to ignore it and moved quickly to my room, packing another box of clothes away.

"There are some discrepancies in Tremaine Marketings books," Agnus sang gleefully, "money is missing that is awfully close that the amounts the FBI was inquiring about." It felt as if a needle entered my heart. I continued packing while she leaned against the door frame obviously wanting to see my reaction. I did my best not to give her one.

"Embezzling is an awful, awful crime," Agnus continued, "I tried to make it clear to them that my daughter wouldn't have anything to do with that." There was a chuckle in her voice. I continued packing, praying she hadn't connected Raj to me.

"I told them that type of crime would get you fired," Agnus added, "and as no longer an employee of Tremaine Marketing, you would lose all rights to inherit the firm." I turned my head to her and cringed at her smile. "Those rights would fall to me as your father's next heir." I couldn't control my tongue.

"Bitch!" The company was my last tie to my father. It was his legacy and my duty to see that it remained strong. Why he ever put Agnus between me and that legacy was still lost on me.

"I'll take that as a guilty plea," Agnus laughed. Damn my mouth. She would delve deeper. If she uncovered Raj's complicity everything would unravel. I sped up my packing. I had to preempt Agnus. It would cost a large chunk of my inheritance, but I had Peter. He was worth more than a hundred companies. Sorry dad, I hope Agnus was worth it.

The weight of the defeat hit hard when I exited the house under Agnus' gleeful stare. I had wasted many years struggling to maintain my temper. Working impossible hours trying to outlast the bitch. It had been a waste. I tried to think of Peter and all I had gained. I needed his arms to quell the pain. He was in meetings again, so I wouldn't seem him until much later. The tears came while I waited at a red light. I had failed my father. It was his fault, but I failed nonetheless.

I pulled over into a big box store parking lot. Leaning my head on the steering wheel, I tried to slow my heart and stem the tears. I had cried too much over all that had happened. This was just something I had to let go of. The golddigger would be out of my life. I should be happy with that consolation prize. I was startled by a soft knock on my window. William was there, his face full of concern. I had forgotten my tail.

"I'm sorry, William," I said, after wiping my eyes. Frank was on the other side of the car, looking for some kind of threat I suspect, "I forgot you guys were there."

"You're not supposed to know," William chuckled. At least his humor made me feel better. I stepped out of the car when Frank came around.

"I just had some bad news is all," I said, talking to them like we were friends, "I screwed up a lot of things when I went to that dance."

"You seem happy enough with Mr. Charming," Frank injected.

"Yes, I do have him and wouldn't trade it for anything," I smiled, "It's just some of the costs are higher than I wished. I think I just lost my father's business."

"How's that?" William asked. I explained to them what I could, leaving Raj out of it. The will, embezzling my own money, and the probable cost of being so foolish.

"Agnus sounds like a Bitch," William commented.

"That's what I called her. Probably not a good thing to say given the circumstances." Frank laughed at my words. At least sharing my pain made me feel a little better. Sometimes you just need to put a voice to it and let some of it burn off. I laughed with him.

"Are you going to be all right?" Frank asked.

"I think so," I replied, "this is the second time I'm grateful to you guys." I surprised Frank by giving him a hug. I followed with William who hugged me back. I am sure I just violated a whole bunch of FBI rules. They could just tack it onto my sentence. At least the guys were smiling when they headed to their car and I was done with my self-admonishment. No point in second guessing if I can't have a do-over.

I called Brendan as soon as I got home. I hated leaving my lawyers in the dark, but I also didn't want them exposed to ethical dilemmas. I informed him where the money for the cotillion ticket, limo and hair-dresser came from. He seemed to take it in stride, asking some probing questions to clarify issues. He was most interested in the dollar amounts and the provisions of the trust my father had saddled me with. I clarified what I could and he promised me everything would be alright. I was surprised when I found out that I wouldn't be taking the stand. "Some rights are best exercised," Brendan insisted. The Charmings trusted him, so did I.

Peter and I had been slowly switching our internal clocks. Since I didn't have my night work, he began working during the day and spent evenings with me like non-vampires. His abundance of meetings made me feel guilty. I was sure I had greatly wounded his business and healing it was taking an enormous amount of time. He assured me I hadn't done anything he couldn't handle. Every night, he would erase my doubts with love. I always found them again when he left the next morning.

The night before my trial was especially tense. I had spent the day feeling I had lost control of my life. Rebecca had called to say that she and Daniel would be in court for support. I was glad of the diversion her call gave me. Too much time to think is not good for the condemned. Peter had cleared his afternoon so he could spend it with me. He sensed my apprehension when he left that morning. I had to practically shove him out the door. I knew he had an important meeting first thing. I placated myself by playing a house-wife. I cleaned and made a salad for lunch. I hated being a housewife.

I was busy cutting carrots when I felt a kiss on the back of my neck. Peter had snuck in and was rather pleased with his stealth. I turned into him and all the bad things in the world drained away. In each other's arms, we were unstoppable.

"Whatever happens tomorrow, know that I love you," I whispered once my lips had tasted him.

"And I you, no matter what happens tomorrow, or the next day, or the one after that," Peter added.

"So, I am screwed next week," I joked. We could always turn silly words into laughter. Peter lifted me off the floor with a deep hug, then reached past me to grab a piece of carrot.

"You were screwed the moment I met you," Peter said, throwing the carrot in his mouth, "now you're stuck with me." I kissed him, not caring that he was munching on the carrot. He reached for another piece and I slapped his hand playfully.

"Wait," I said, "let me put some in the salad." He laughed, backed away and held up the piece I thought I had stopped him from taking. "Salad," I demanded, pointing at the bowl full of salad. His eyebrows bounced and tossed the carrot into his mouth. Men! I dropped the knife on the counter and tackled him.

Peter let me win the brief wrestling match. I liked being on top, in control. Weeks of bowing to things out of my control and now I had the man I loved beneath me. He reached up slowly, some attempt to bring me closer. I took his wrist and pushed it back to his side. I lowered my head, my smile meeting his, and gave him my love. I felt his resistance fade, muscles relaxing. I broke the kiss and began unbuttoning his shirt.

"I am yours," Peter smiled. I tried not to laugh at the small speck of carrot in his teeth. I kissed the carrot away while I went to work on his buttons. Peter sensed my desire and allowed me to control our love. My lips found his secrets as he had found mine. It was the first time he had given up everything. We had shared often, but this time it was me giving pleasure and expecting nothing in return except tacit obedience. For a short while, I was the most powerful person in the room. Peter had given me his strength and I needed it more than he knew.

"I need to come home early more often," Peter whispered. I could feel his heart slowing as I lay on his chest.

"I don't want to be just a housewife," I said. I wanted Peter, but I also wanted something of my own. It was as good a time as any to clear things up, now that I had some strength back. I could feel Peter holding back a chuckle. I looked up, thinking he found my statement funny.

"You don't need my permission," Peter said, "though...if I disagree...does that mean I have a chance of getting tackled again?" The little boy whimsy in his eyes made me laugh. I slapped his shoulder and he feigned pain making me laugh harder.

"I just wanted you to know. I'm not sure how you see our future."

"I want you," Peter said, rolling me to my side, "I can hire a maid."

"I don't want to disappoint you. I have no idea what you're expecting and..."

"You," Peter repeated, his hand lovingly caressing my neck, "I am expecting you and no one else. I have the same worries, but every time I kiss you, they fade away. So I figured, I just need to keep kissing you." I loved when he was like this. Playful and meaningful at the same time. He was correct, kissing solved a lot of issues.

~

$\mathcal{W}$ alking into the courtroom was surreal. I had seen it on TV and been on a few tours in grade school. The one time I had been selected for jury duty, I was never called to serve. As a defendant, it was an imposing room. I walked in with my lawyers, hopefully presenting an imposing sight myself. I refused to look meek. If they were going to take me down, then it would be with a straight back and a proud face. Enough with the self-pity. I would take my lumps, solve the problem and continue the next chapter of my life. The chapter entitled 'Peter.'

I was surprised to see Jaq and Gus seated in one of the rows. The FBI must have been busy tracking down all my transgressions. Gus waved with a flirty look in his eyes. Jaq smiled. I felt bad for them being dragged to my trial. The thought that their pay might be retracted as stolen funds sent a chill through me. That would have to be rectified. Another debt.

My fears were confirmed when I saw Daphne and Beatrice in another row. I tried to give them an apologetic expression. It probably came off as stupid mixed with insanity. They didn't shy away and gave me friendly smiles.

Rebecca and Daniel were all smiles. They had an aura of confidence I didn't share. Ruth and Betty sat next to them. Ruth with a polite nod and Betty with a thumbs up.

Right behind what I suspected was the prosecutor was Agnus. She was smiling ear to ear. It was the most unfriendly thing I had ever seen. I had a brief unhealthy desire to claw it off her face. Thankfully, I buried the thought with the idea that this might be the last time I ever see her. She would get what she wanted and I would have Peter and a new life.

My lawyers and I sat at a large wooden table that mirrored the prosecutor's table on the other side of the room. I took a deep breath and straightened in my chair. Brendan conferred quietly with Mary, another of my counsel, and she passed down a set of papers. Brendan looked at them a moment then pushed them down the table to me.

"We took the liberty of handling your taxes this year," Brendan whispered, "if you could sign these, it will help in your defense." I looked down at the stack a papers in front of me. I usually only had a couple of sheets when I did my taxes. This was at least twenty pages of IRS forms. There were two sign-here stickers poking out the right side. Brendan smiled and I felt his confidence. I shrugged my shoulders and signed. Mary stood, gathered the document and headed out to make copies. At least my taxes were done. One headache not to worry about.

We stood when the judge arrived. Judge Manfred was black-gowned with a round face and gray beard that reminded me of a well trimmed Santa Claus. He didn't smile like Santa when the charges were read. In fact, it looked like humor was foreign to him. I sat back down and listened to a slew of perfunctory statements on both sides. The trial began in earnest with the first witness.

The first witness was Peter. I cringed when his name was called. I should have expected it since it was his team that first recognized the breach. He smiled to me as he walked from behind me. I hadn't seen him walk in. I lost track of him when my lawyers briefed me on what to expect.

Peter took the witness stand. He looked adorable. I scrunched my eyes, trying to separate the naked Peter from the one in the chair. I couldn't, so I smiled at him. I received a loving smile in return. The prosecutor was staring at me with an expression that didn't contain any love. I guess I was compromising his witness. Peter winked at me and then became serious, stating his name and promising to tell the truth.

"On the night of..." The prosecutor began, describing the events that were undisputed fact before he hit on a question. "did you identify a breach of the Shark firewall?"

"Yes," Peter said and didn't elaborate. I knew he wouldn't lie, but he had no intention of helping the man. I liked Peter in his suit. When he wasn't smiling at me, he was the picture of authority and strength. His power weakened greatly when he smiled. He became approachable. I looked over to the jury. I had a flash of jealousy when I saw the eyes of the four women jurors. They were fixed on Peter. My Peter. I had to look away. They were supposed to be looking at him. I straightened my back and returned my mind to the proceedings.

"How did you identify the incursion?" The prosecutor's question was followed by a long list of technical procedures that would have bored Bill Gates. I could see the jurors eyes glaze over as Peter used acronyms and long-winded techno jargon with abandon. Twice the prosecutor tried to interrupt, but Peter wasn't having it. By the time he was done, we all realized that he was highly skilled and we had no idea how he identified the incursion.

"How would you categorize this assault?" the prosecutor asked.

"I'm not sure I understand the question," Peter responded. He was so cute when he played dumb. Somehow he could change his eyes from intense to innocent in a heartbeat.

"Amateur, skilled, highly skilled?" the prosecutor clarified.

"It was the most sophisticated attack I have ever seen," Peter said. He was looking near the prosecutor's table when he said it, almost as if he was answering the question for someone else. I turned my head and glanced toward the table. There was an older man in a blue air force uniform with a star on the color. General Rickers, I assumed.

"In your opinion, would the development of this attack take the resources of a government to design and execute?" The question was followed by a series of objections that were overruled by the judge who followed up with instructions to the jury that Peter's response would be an opinion of an expert and not necessarily fact.

"No." Peter's answer took the prosecutor by surprise. He looked down at this notes, then back at his table where his assistant shrugged his shoulder.

"We have depositions that state you have claimed that only a foreign government had the capability to develop such an attack."

"Yes," Peter said calmly, "I know longer feel that is the case. I was rather...upset when I made those assumptions."

"So, you want this court to believe that an individual has developed, in your words, the most sophisticated attack you have ever seen?"

"As his honor has stated, it is only my opinion," Peter said. Again, he was speaking to Rickers. The prosecutor walked back to his desk and conferred with his assistant for a moment. Rickers leaned into the conversation. Then a third joined, Agent Stratford. I felt my bladder contract. The judge called the prosecutor back to the questioning after a moment.

"What is your relationship with the defendant?" Peter considered the question then looked directly at me.

"I intend to ask her to be my wife when this is over." I heard Rebecca audibly gasp at Peter's response. My heart nearly burst.

"Yes," I answered the unasked question. I wasn't thinking about where I was when it came out. All I saw was Peter looking at me. All I saw was love. The pounding of the gavel and the commotion of the courtroom was lost on us. The rest of the world could fall into a bottomless pit for all I cared.

"Order!" The judge yelled again. This time, I heard the gavel but ignored it. I smiled at my love and nearly melted when he smiled back. It took awhile to bring the courtroom under control as Peter and I continued to absorb each other with our eyes.

"Mr. Charming!" the prosecutor said for the second time. Peter turned away from me and looked questionably at the prosecutor. I couldn't hide my smile and didn't really care who saw it.

"Has your testimony been comprised by your relationship with the defendant?"

"Comprised? No," Peter responded, "though I am sure it has been tainted. Have you ever been in love?" The court broke out in laughter. More gavel pounding and the judge looking less and less like Santa all the time.

"Mr. Charming," the judge instructed, "you are here to answer questions, not ask them."

"Yes, your honor."

"Could your assessment of the capability of the attacker of your firewall be tainted by your relationship with the defendant?"

"Absolutely not," Peter said, "My firewall, and, therefore, the armed force's networks, are completely exposed to the talents of a single individual." General Rickers stood quickly and leaned down to the assistant prosecutor who immediately waved the prosecutor over. The judge rolled his eyes and slammed his gavel down.

"This court does not have tolerance for interference, even by the military," the judge decreed.

"Your honor, may I approach the bench?" the prosecutor asked.

# BRENDAN JOINED THE PROSECUTOR AT THE BENCH

"Lead counsel only." Brendan joined the prosecutor at the bench. There was a bunch of whisperings that seemed more spirited than it should be. I looked over at Peter. Our eyes met and I mouthed 'yes' again. His smile was so wonderful. I didn't need him on his knee. I just needed him.

"There will be a thirty-minute recess while counsel confers in chambers," the judge announced with a tone that sounded less than pleased. Lead counsel and the judge headed through a door behind the bench. The jury was led out by the sergeant at arms.

A soft hand found my shoulder. I turned to see Rebecca, happy tears in her eyes, leaning over the waist high divider.

"Welcome to the family," Rebecca said. I rose and we hugged. I promised myself I wouldn't break down again. I failed.

"Sorry," Peter said from behind me, "I didn't want to commit perjury." I was in his arms before his words were finished.

"Yes," I said again.

"I haven't asked yet."

"Yes," I repeated. I was sure there were rules about the defendant kissing the witness, but there was no one to tell me what they were. More importantly, there was no one stopping me. Whatever happened, Peter was in my arms. Nothing else mattered. I barely heard the clerk call General Rickers into chambers.

"I was planning something more romantic," Peter whispered, "I hope you aren't disappointed."

"I only need you," I whispered back, "we make our own romance."

"Peter Charming!" the clerk called. Peter smiled at me as if he knew the summons was coming.

"They will call you next," Peter told me, "I am throwing a hail mary. Do you trust me?"

"Until I die," I answered. Peter's smile grew as he separated from me and headed to chambers.

I waited for ten minutes. None of the other lawyers could guess what was going on. It was rare when nonlawyers were called into chambers.

"Ella Tremaine." I followed the clerk into the chambers.

"She needs to be under oath," the prosecutor said as I enter the room.

"Cut the crap, Larkin," the judge said, "we are way past formality now." He looked at me and waited for the door to close. "We have reached a point where national security tramples on civil proceedings. I have been informed that you know of an individual who has the capability to compromise the Shark firewall," the judge looked toward General Rickers, "and therefore, the nation's security networks." I looked at Peter and he gave me a small nod. Raj's family was wrapped in the answer I was about to give. I almost lied, but Peter asked for trust.

"Yes," I said as I prayed inside. The judge nodded and then looked at Rickers.

"Given immunity, would this individual be willing to work for Mr. Charming?" Rickers asked.

"Yes," I answered, "and he would only require one thing." My hands were shaking.

"What would that be?" Rickers asked. My next statement was a blind leap of faith. The request would practically paint a target on Raj. I looked at Peter. He smiled and nodded.

"More than anything, he and his family want to be citizens of the United States," I replied. My heart was beating so hard, I was surprised no one else heard it.

"Is he that good?" Rickers asked Peter.

"Ingenious. He thinks way out of the box," Peter replied.

"A foreigner?" Rickers stated more than asked, "I wish I could be certain of his intentions." I closed my eyes, took a deep breath, and leaped.

"The phone from that night has messages from him," I said quietly, hoping I hadn't just signed Raj's family's deportation order, "you can hear it in his voice and read it in his words. He had no intention of attacking America. He and his family love it as much as you and I."

"Where's the phone?" Ricker's asked.

"We were going to submit it as evidence," Larkin answered, "It's on the table, but it's encrypted and NSA hasn't been able to break into it yet."

"I know the password," I admitted. There, I just hung Raj out completely. I was about to hand the prosecution everything.

"Can I see the phone?" Rickers asked. He looked at me and I saw some compassion in his eyes. He was beginning to see what it was costing me. Maybe this was just a dance.

Larkin looked desperately at the judge. He didn't want to give up a piece of physical evidence, especially when I just stated I knew the password.

"Produce the phone," the judge ruled. I could see he didn't like the interference nor the extra time this was taking. Larkin left and shortly returned with the phone in a plastic bag. The judge nodded as Rickers removed the phone from the plastic.

"Password?" Rickers asked. My face went red.

"I can type it in," I said, moving forward.

"No," Larkin jumped in, "if this isn't what you say, I don't want the phone tampered with."

"The password, Ms. Tremaine," the judge said, agreeing with Larkin. I looked at the five men in the room and thought I would die.

"Can I whisper it?" I begged Rickers. The curious looks I got made it all worse. Rickers looked to the judge.

"Yes," the judge said. I was blushing horrible when I leaned toward Rickers' ear.I couldn't believe I had to do this. I should have chosen a different password.

"Peter likes my breasts," I whispered so only Rickers would hear it, "no spaces." Rickers eyes shot to Peter and he struggled to keep the corner of his lips down. "It was from before," I defended the password, "the flat tire, before I knew Peter was Peter Charming." Rickers lips were straining as he typed in the code. The phone let him in and he looked back at me. He knew then, before he even read the texts, it was only a dance.

We watched as Rickers scrolled through the texts. He fired off one of the voicemails and held it to his ear. The humor in his eyes grew as he listened to another. Raj confessing to missing the logs and begging my forgiveness, praying that his stupidity didn't get me in trouble.

"You say the NSA couldn't break this man's encryption?" Rickers asked Larkin. Larkin shook his head no. Rickers smiled at me.

"It really was just a dance," Rickers stated. I nodded my head. "This phone and its encryption are also considered a national security issue." Rickers told the judge. The judge nodded.

"So, you'll get him and his family citizenship?" I asked desperately.

"Done," Rickers told me, "Charming will handle the logistics. Nothing of this leaves this room." He directed the last statement to the prosecutor.

"The wire fraud still exists," Larkin said. The judge looked at me.

"Legally, that is correct," the judge said to me, "if it is determined you are a participant of the fraud, you will not be able to bring up the aforementioned individual. You will stand alone." He looked at the prosecutor, "you will have to refrain from any mention of a third party."

"I agree," I said with a smile. Raj was out of it and his family was safe. Espionage was off the table.

"You don't have a choice," the judge said. I saw his lips curl for the briefest moment. Maybe he did have a little Santa in him.

I left the chamber floating on a cloud. Though I wasn't wearing a ring, I was engaged to the only person in the world who I truly loved, Raj and his family were safe, and I was only on trial for wire fraud. What a wonderful turn of events.

The trial began again with the judge instructing the court to ignore all references to the Shark firewall and the skill level of the person or persons who comprised the network or networks. I watched the jurors eyes glaze over again. Peter was once again seated in the witness chair and the prosecutor continued his questioning.

"Were you responsible for the children's hospital charity cotillion website?"

"Yes."

"Were your systems the target of fraudulent activity prior to the cotillion?"

"No." Peter held a straight face. The prosecutor's face was starting to look a little flush.

"No one compromised your system?" the prosecutor asked.

"I believe someone did find what you would call a backdoor into to the network." Peter clarified.

"So, fraud was perpetrated," the prosecutor said exasperatedly.

"No."

"Either they broke in or they didn't, Which is it Mr. Charming?"

"Someone definitely entered the network in an unexpected way," Peter answered with a straight face.

"You do not consider that fraud?"

"No. No data was taken, altered or deleted. A ticket was inserted into the database and the charity received the prescribed payment for that ticket." Peter let a small chuckle, "I'm not sure why they just didn't use the standard web interface. The results would have been the same." he paused for a moment then added, "I saw no fraud, just an unorthodox transaction."

"What was the price of that ticket?"

"$5,000."

"No more questions," the prosecutor spat as he returned to his table. A hushed conference between his assistant and the Agent Stratford.

"Cross-exam?" the judge asked.

"No questions at this time," Brendan announced. Peter was excused. We shared a smile as he moved to a seat directly behind me. I liked having him close.

A representative for Coupon Crave was called next. He was unaware of any unauthorized intrusions to his company's network. He was most adamant that everyone in the courtroom knew that they take enormous care of their customers data. I had to smile at Raj's skill.

Jaq and Beatrice were called in turn. They were both adamant that they had received full payment from Coupon Crave and controlled no networks. They were both asked the price of their services to me. I smelled a trap in the dollar amounts. I conferred quietly with Brendan who just nodded and said it will be alright.

Agnus was called to the stand next. She didn't even try to hide her pleased smile.

"You heard the previous testimony of the purchases made and received by Ella Tremaine?" the prosecutor asked.

"Yes I did," Agnus answered. She looked at me as she answered. She was enjoying this.

"Are those dollar amounts familiar?" the prosecutor prodded.

"Yes, they are," Agnus announced, "they are the exact amounts missing from a company account." The prosecutor walked over to his table and grabbed a set of papers.

"Here is the independently audited transaction log for the account mentioned. I would like to submit it as exhibit A." There were no objections, which surprised me, and it was placed in evidence.

"Did you authorize a disbursement of those amounts?"

"No, I did not."

"Did any other authorized person disburse those amounts?"

"No," Agnus replied. Her grin was growing.

"What do you think happened to those funds?" the prosecutor

asked. Brendan stopped one of my other lawyers from objecting. He seemed comfortable with the line of questioning. I wasn't.

"I think it was stolen by Ella Tremaine," Agnus said. The words came from her mouth like music. Her happiness was apparent to everyone in the room. She was rattling my nerves.

"No more questions."

"Cross-exam?" the judge asked. Brendan rose confidently and moved toward Agnus.

"Mrs. Tremaine, what is your relationship to Ella Tremaine?"

"I am her stepmother."

"What is your legal relationship with Ella Tremaine?"

"I am the executor of her father's will," Agnus said confidently, "the trustee of the assets until Ella is 32."

"What assets would those be?"

"Tremaine Marketing, Inc, a few bank accounts, a house and some stock holdings," Agnus said, her confidence wavering. Brendan nodded.

"Did Ella Tremaine mention the cotillion prior to the event?"

"I'm not sure?" Agnus lied.

"We could call your daughters to the stand to help your memory," Brendan said.

"Oh yes, I do remember having a discussion pertaining to the event."

"Did Ella Tremaine express interest in going to the cotillion?"

"I'm not sure I remember," Agnus lied again. At least her smile had disappeared. I liked nervous Agnus.

"Again, would your daughter's memory be more complete?"

"Yes, now I remember. She did express interest." I think I saw sweat on her forehead.

"What was your answer to that request?"

"I...I believe I didn't think it prudent," Agnus stuttered.

"Who from Tremaine Marketing did go to the cotillion?"

"If memory serves, Anastasia and Drizella, and myself, " Agnus said slowly.

"Who are they?"

"Sales representatives for Tremaine Marketing."

"What is their relationship to Ella Tremaine?"

"Stepsisters," Agnus said after an uncomfortable pause.

"So, to summarize, you disallowed Ella to use her own company's money to attend the cotillion because you thought it not prudent." Brendan paused for a moment, rubbing his chin as if he was trying to understand, "but you thought it prudent to use Ella's company money to send your daughters to the same cotillion."

"It was a business decision," Agnus justified, "my daughters were representing the firm."

"You sent two sales representatives instead of an owner?"

"Ella doesn't own Tremaine Marketing until she is 32," Angus countered.

"No, I believe the law would disagree with you. You are the trustee, not the temporary owner. You have a fiduciary responsibility to represent Ella Tremaine as if she was 32."

"She can't just take money," Agnus argued.

"The amount is immaterial to the total worth of the company. More of a mistaken withdraw than a theft. She has declared it on her taxes as dispersed earnings." Brendan walked over to our table and grabbed a copy of the tax form I had just signed. "A minor disbursement from her own company declared legally to the IRS. I do believe the error lies with your fiduciary responsibility, not with such a small disbursement she is entitled to anyway." Agnus was visibly perturbed.

"I would like to note that my own compensation had to be paid by a third party," Brendan continued, "since Ella Tremaine's trustee refused to release funds for Ella's defense."

"I am failing to see a crime here," the judge said, "I am beginning to see a breach of trust that precipitated the events. Larkin is there any evidence that the money in question was not ultimately Ella Tremaine's? Are there any victims beside Ella Tremaine."

The prosecutor was in a conference with Agent Stratford and his assistant.

"Larkin?" the judge repeated himself.

"There may be," the prosecutor stated, "the funds in question resided in a US bank. Depending upon how those funds were accessed, it could very well represent a crime." The judge rolled his eyes.

"Agnus Tremaine, you are excused," the judge said, "I would recommend you find legal counsel of your own. I doubt your decisions as executor will stand up to legal scrutiny."

"There will be a two-hour recess," the judge continued, "after which the prosecution will have to convince me there is a reason to continue this trial." The gavel came down and the judge left quickly.

I turned to Peter and found him gone. Rebecca shrugged her shoulders and pointed at the door. I walked out to the hall and didn't seem him. I couldn't believe he left me. He just sort of asked me to marry him and he disappears. I wanted my sort-of fiancee.

Peter came up the stairs, a smile across his face. I jumped into his arms and tasted his wonderful lips.

"Where did you go?" I asked.

"Picking up some leverage," Peter answered cryptically.

"I already said yes. What do you need leverage for?" I joked.

"Not for you. For her," Peter said, pointing at agent Stratford. He split away from me and went directly to Stratford and directed her to the side, away from others. He pulled out his phone and showed her something that made her face lose its color. They had a brief heated conversation that never rose above a whisper though the faces said they were yelling. After a moment, Peter came back smiling.

"Looks like it will end now," Peter said. I wrapped him in my arms.

"And why is that?"

"Someone, protected by immunity, happened to locate some security camera footage on FBI servers that was not supposed to exist," Peter said.

"Oh god," I said, "Raj didn't see it, did he?" Peter pulled me close.

"He loves you," Peter soothed, "not as much as me, but enough to forget."

"You saw it?"

"Yes."

"It's embarrassing," I admitted shyly. Peter's hand caressed the side of my face, his eyes caressing my soul.

"Nothing is embarrassing between us," Peter said before he kissed me. It was still embarrassing, but I could ignore it.

Peter's parents took us out to lunch. Rebecca scolded Peter for announcing a pending proposal without the proper romantic setup, especially a ring. I assured her, I was more than willing to wait. I started that morning believing there was a good chance I would have to spend some time in prison. Now, it was looking like I might get away with a slap on the wrist and gain a husband to boot.

Daniel rolled his eyes as Rebecca and I started preliminary talk on wedding arrangements. I had no desire for Agnus to participate, so that left me with only one woman to lean on. I knew Peter would just nod his head and say yes to everything, Rebecca on the other hand, had the style and the desire to make it wonderful. I didn't want a big wedding, but I did want it wonderful.

"What do you think about a garden wedding, Peter?" Rebecca asked. I had already agreed that it sounded wonderful.

"That sounds like a good idea," Peter said, nodding his head. True to form. He turned back to the discussion he was having with his father.

"What about using The Fountains, Peter? Somewhere along the walking trail." Rebecca pushed. I smiled, expecting acquiescence followed by a nod. He seemed deeply entrenched into the conversation with his father.

"Yes," Peter agreed, turning to his mother, "but it has to be by that small fountain. The one with the little cement ducks." He returned to his father.

"But there are better spots on the grounds," Rebecca countered, "like the corner with willow trees or the tiered flower beds." Peter turned to me.

"'I believe we shared our first kiss by the ducks," Peter said. I smiled at the look in his eyes. There was all the romance I needed right there.

"By the ducks," I agreed.

"Oh," Rebecca said, her smile mirroring ours, "then it must be by the ducks." Daniel chuckled at his wife's quick change of heart.

"Why don't you wait until it's official, Rebecca," Daniel said, "the girl doesn't even have her ring yet." That comment was followed by a brief discussion on the idiocy of men. I half-heartedly sided with Rebecca. Peter, of course, was the exception to the rule.

~

*J*udge Manfred looked less than pleased at the prosecutor. Agent Stratford and Larkin were in a heated discussion. Another man in a suit, next to Stratford, seemed to be supporting her argument.

"You have had sufficient time, counselor," the judge growled, "I do not appreciate you wasting the court's time as well." Larkin turned, his face poorly masking his anger.

"At this time, your honor," Larkin's words seemed to struggle out of his mouth, "we lack sufficient evidence to proceed with prosecution." Both Stratford and the man next to her sat down, staring straight ahead. Agnus, sitting behind them, looked pale. I was feeling much better.

"I would like to make a motion to dismiss," Brendan said quickly as he stood. My legs felt all jittery as the excitement began to creep up my spine.

"Does the prosecution take issue with that?" the Judge asked.

"No your honor," Larkin said quietly.

"Case dismissed!" the judge announced and slammed his gavel down. A smile appeared on his face as he looked at me. I smiled back at Santa. "I am a Justice of the Peace," he continued, looking at me, "if you are ever in need." He winked and headed off to his chambers.

Peter wrapped me in his arms before I could turn around. The world disappeared as we kissed. I had to force him away so I could thank my lawyers. Each getting a hug and my gratitude. Peter followed with handshakes and his gratitude. I was free.

Rebecca and Daniel joined us in the hall outside of the courtroom. More hugging and shared joy. I saw William and Frank coming toward me, smiles on their faces.

"Peter, this is William and Frank," I said, "our Tom and Jerry." Frank laughed as Peter shook his hand and then moved to William.

"Helping Ella with Rayburn," Peter said, shaking his head, "I owe you guys for that."

"Forget it," William returned, "it broke up an otherwise dull day."

I mouthed 'I'll tell you later' to Rebecca who looked fairly confused over the conversation.

"So, you two are getting married?" Frank asked, his finger moving between Peter and I.

"Yes," I replied happily, pulling Peter next to me, "It kind of made this all worthwhile." I saw Frank look past me. I followed his eyes and saw Agnus leaving the courtroom. Frank traded a look with William and nodded his head toward Agnus. William moved quickly.

"We have an early wedding present for you," Frank smiled and quickly followed William. They approached Agnus with badges out.

"Agnus Tremaine," William announced loudly, "you're under arrest for fraud and conspiracy to commit the same." I covered my mouth as Agnus made a move to run away. In heels, she was no match for Frank.

"What's going on?" Peter asked me.

"I have no idea," I admitted. Agnus was handcuffed, her mouth spilling vulgarities at Frank and William. I had never heard her completely lose it before. She was never the image of purity, but now she sounded like a drunken street walker. Frank sat her down on a bench and began reading her her rights. She was shaking her head, demanding to be let go. William just smiled and walked back over to us.

"White collar crime is our beat," William said proudly.

"What just happened?" I asked.

"After what you told us about Agnus, Frank did a little investigating," William reported, pointing at Frank, "we are quite familiar with her lawyer." William put air quotes around the word 'lawyer.' "A little bit of questioning, some deal making and he sang like a bird."

"What did she do?" Peter asked.

"Why, altered your father's will to suit her needs," William said, looking at me. My father didn't screw me. That bitch did.

"Oh, my!" Rebecca said. Peter pulled me close, allowing me to borrow his strength. Wonderful thoughts of my father not intentionally leaving me to that woman began to be replaced by an anger. The things I began to think were awful and the handcuffs on Agnus made them seem doable. I looked up at Peter and he squeezed me in his arms. The anger dissipated and a smile formed. I took Peter by the hand and marched over to Agnus. Frank, thinking the worst, stepped in front of Agnus to protect his prisoner. I smiled at him and he relaxed.

"Thank you, Agnus," I said sweetly, as if I was talking to someone I cared about, "without you, I would have never found Peter." I watched her fume on the bench, looking everywhere but at me.

"Whiney bitch," Angus whispered to the wall.

"By the way," I said clearly, "you're fired." It was my company now and I didn't have to wait seven more years.

"I don't think we should invite her to the wedding," Peter said. I laughed.

"Frank, I hope you and William will come," I added.

"We wouldn't miss it," Frank replied, "you think you'll have more of that calamari there?" Peter laughed.

~

he wedding was a beautiful thing. Rebecca had pulled out all the stops. Everyone I loved was there, including three new US citizens. Kiran was my maid of honor and Aanya beside her. George stood for Peter, which had surprised me. I didn't know they were such good friends, though the idea of seeing George in the future pleased me. He had such a wonderful happiness about him. Raj stood in for my father and walked me down the aisle, or a walking path in our case. Judge Manfred was true to his word and presided happily.

Rebecca cried throughout the whole ceremony. I, for once, did not. I knew what I wanted and it was called Peter. There was nothing standing in the way anymore. When I said 'I do' it was clear and I made sure everyone heard it. Peter didn't stop smiling through the whole proceeding, almost as if he had a secret. I found it delightfully charming.

The Fountains was decked out for the reception. Food was in abundance, including a tray filled with calamari. Daniel contributed by locating the FBI logo and affixing to the side of the tray. The smiles it brought to Frank and William was worth Rebecca's scorn for having something out of place.

"So, I understand Tremaine Marketing was officially transferred to you yesterday," George mentioned as we gathered at the head table. I took Peter's hand in mine. I really liked being married.

Walking into the special board meeting, yesterday, seemed like a dream. The board members congratulating me, then looking shocked when I began to list the changes that were to occur. I shifted funds to the east coast where sales had been dropping off, enacted bonus adjustments that reflect actual profit gains, not status quo, and informed them of the need to replace Raj. They expected a girl and found a strong woman instead. It was exhilarating.

"Signed and sealed," I replied, "exactly how my dad wanted it." I looked at Peter, "he really would have liked you." Peter leaned in for a kiss. One of many that day. I saw George jerk suddenly and sit up straighter.

"Ahem...how will you balance work with a family?" George asked. It sounded foreign coming out of his mouth. Rebecca was sitting next to him, looking away with feigned indifference. I smiled knowing that George was Rebecca's patsy. It was Peter who answered.

"We've decided against children," Peter said as serious as possible, "they cry too much and there aren't enough qualified babysitters." I kicked him under the table for teasing his mother.

"I could babysit," Rebecca said in a panic before she realized that Peter was teasing her. The idea of a grandchild was plastered all over her face. I rose and walked over while Peter laughed.

"We think two is a good number," I whispered in Rebecca's ear. Peter and I had already had the conversation.

"Oh!" Rebecca said, her smile spanning the room. It was for her ears only and she kept it there. I sat back down, sharing a few more smiles with my mother in-law. She was now as happy as I was. Peter gave me another kiss, which I returned more passionately than I should in public.

After dinner, the band started warming up. Rebecca had mentioned that she wanted to see Peter dance again, and for once, he would be required. I didn't care that he lacked agility and grace. It would be our first dance as a married couple. His awkwardness would probably make it our last dance together, which was something I could live with. At least I would have tonight.

Peter rose when they called us out. He took my hand confidently with a smile and led me to the floor. I knew how difficult that was for him. That he went willing, spoke well of his love. I followed him, mirroring his smile. Preparing to compensate for his lack of skill. I suspected I would have to lead.

"I have a confession to make," Peter whispered, once we were on the floor.

"Yes?"

"Those meetings I have had to attend lately weren't really meetings," Peter sighed, "I have been secretly seeing a lot of George lately and we've gotten pretty close." Stupid thoughts ran through my head as Peter took my lead hand in his and placed his other on around my waist.

"What?" I asked, trying to understand. I tried to shake off the stupid thoughts. Peter smiled.

"He's taught me to dance, my love," Peter said, humor and love in his eyes. The music started and he stepped off, leading me with a grace I didn't know he possessed. He danced like a prince.

Made in the USA
Middletown, DE
18 September 2020